Old Soldiers Never Die

WOLF MANKOWITZ

Old Soldiers Never Die

An Atlantic Monthly Press Book
BOSTON · Little, Brown and Company · TORONTO

PR
6025
A4755
.m8

ATLANTIC–LITTLE, BROWN BOOKS
ARE PUBLISHED BY
LITTLE, BROWN AND COMPANY
IN ASSOCIATION WITH
THE ATLANTIC MONTHLY PRESS

37222

A.R.P., the initials of the Air Raid Precautions organization in Britain during the Second World War, a voluntary civil-defence army which fought a nightly Mons in the London streets — to its veterans and all disabled soldiers this book is dedicated.

Old Soldiers Never Die

I

EVERYBODY thought Arp was just a rubbish-picker, but that's all they knew, the dustman who tipped the rubbish on to the dump, so untidy you didn't know where to start picking, and the Old Cock who looked after the dump, and Rambam the dealer who bought Arp's rubbish from him (what he didn't decide to keep for a rainy day, that was). All of them thought Arp was just a plain rubbish-picker.

He had to laugh. He opened his mouth to laugh. He laughed inside his stomach, lungs, even so near as his throat. And then Arp got annoyed with himself for bothering, for even trying, for being so stupid to forget such a thing, standing there in front of a person his mouth open like a fool, the sound of the laugh just fighting to come through. For in the end it didn't. It got

[3]

swallowed back behind that small black space while his lips and jaw-bone just jumped about and the stupid fat tongue lolled useless and people thought he was stuttering and so waited, but then suddenly looked away and walked on because they could see Arp was dumb.

He wore these big knobbly boots with irons, the clay dry on them, leaving a clanging crumbling white footmark track, or if it was wet they hung at the ends of his legs, two dead lead lumps. But he kept them well greased with lard and they came up good as new no matter what clay ditches by what mountains of mouldering junk steaming in the early morning sunshine he dragged through and over, his quite clean carefully mended sack empty over his shoulder, the knobbly boots kicking their way forward till it was late afternoon and the sack was full of empty bottles, and bones and bits of metal, all stamped down by his trusty iron-shod feet. Arp also carried (separately) dry cardboard boxes pressed flat and tied into a neat parcel with a coil of string kept special for the purpose.

But what did *they* know apart from all that, the laugh not coming out and the rubbish picking? Arp could talk once just as loud and just as well as the rest of them. And now he couldn't. So he had something over them (if you looked at it fairly) because he knew what it was like to be dumb which is more than they did. It would be good though (it would make them feel small) it would be *very* good though, if only Arp could remember about when he could talk. It was on the tip of his mind even now, but it always slipped back down that little black space, just like his voice did, sort of peeped up and started to creep forward like the Old Cock's tape-worm that he was always on about. Then nipped back before he could speak. Arp's voice that was, not the tape-worm, although they too were dumb like Arp was now.

But anyhow, cutting the same old long story short, here was Arp dragging his old boots over the same old rubbish dump, getting on with his work and minding his own business, and a penny to a pound you would never guess in a million years what that work was. As for why he was doing it, Arp could never remember, although often he stayed awake bedded down in the Nissen hut thinking and thinking why, how. The job started like this.

He came out of a long black tunnel, so long

no one could see (even if they wanted to and Arp for one didn't) the back far end of it. When he came out this end he was standing on a high dump. When he looked round, the whole world was nothing but these rubbish dumps, big and small, the whole world nothing but a lot of rubbish and rubble and bits and pieces and litter and broken cups and chair-seats with the springs coming out and a doll's head and a valuable copper ball-cock. And because all his life (including when he could talk) Arp was always first and foremost a tidy man, spick and span with his clothes, shoes, one of the closest shavers ever, one who had always found a place for everything, he looked round the untidy world and the tears ran down his face, for days and days. The tears ran down among the rubbish dumps, the rain mixed with them, little rivers started to run and wash passages between the smoking heaps.

Then it stopped raining and Arp stopped crying. He felt dead cold, his clothes stiff and cold and damp like a dead cat. But he knew what the job was now. He found a sack and washed it out, and as soon as it dried he started work, and since then he had never looked back. And this was the job Arp had to do. This job was his. The job was simply to tidy up the world which was all these dumps of rubbish, and Arp was the right man for the job.

It would be good if he could tell a few others what it was, but for special reasons the powers-that-be didn't want it to get around, maybe because if too many knew and it leaked out, the ones who got the whole world into such a mess in the first place might start all over again making rubbish out of everything, the entire world a rubbish dump. And if they did, frankly it would be too much for Arp to cope with because even after a good long time now (how long exactly just slipped his mind for the moment) he still hadn't finished clearing up this one rubbish dump. The Old Cock reckoned he never would get through it. "I been looking after it long enough," he said, "and it still surprises me what you can dig out of it." The Old Cock reckoned it one of the finest dumps in the country, and he should know, being in the council service since early in the war when manpower was so short they took on anyone who could twitch. "Pick away, me old Arp," he said, "there's enough here to keep you going, poor old dumb bastard, pick away. At least you don't have a tape-worm."

It was by courtesy of the Old Cock (who had the two jobs for the council, one, keeping an eye on the rubbish dump, and two, guarding the old empty film studios adjoining) that Arp got fixed up with the Nissen hut, back of Ancient Rome.

"I'd give you the Wild West Saloon," the Old Cock said as he showed Arp over the crumbling place — an elephants' graveyard of old romances, "the Double Ace Bar, but it's only a bit of a lean-to that was knocked up very poorly, and it's a bit parky when the rain comes straight through. You could have the gondola. A bloke did one winter but he froze red raw to the marrow with the wind blowing from the allotments. Take the Nissen — it's not pretty, but if you stuff up the windows with some rag and cardboard, you can make yourself snug as a bug. Needs must, as we soon found out first time we took over the trenches from the Frogs at Houplines, before the sand-bag come into its own that was, their losses was so heavy they was just scrubbing up a bit of earth between the dead like a living barrier only dead. When we come out of that lot the one thing I prayed for was a new pair of pants, me own being skin tight and rigid with crawlers. Still, as luck would have it

first scrounge me and Taffy went on I find meself a big pair of pink bloomers. Taffy said I
looked sweet enough to kiss, but they just give
the crawlers their opportunity as it turned out.
Same thing with the Nissen. It's got its draw-
backs but with respect to the Double Ace Bar
it's bloomers to a worn-out pair of underpants.

"Shame," ran on the gabby old soldier as they
walked past Ancient Rome. "Them lovely columns is just eaten up by the weather. It's all
plaster, but it cost a fortune in its day. Will you
take the Nissen?" So Arp took the Nissen for two
shillings a week (off the record) to the Old Cock.

It took Arp three days working solid to clean
up the place. He even found an old pail of blue
distemper, hard as brick, and worked it loose and
gave the whole place out and in a couple of coats.
He fixed the windows with a few pieces of red
and green glass from Westminster Abbey. He
mended the floor with salvaged nails and clapboard from the Wild West Saloon. He got the
little old stove working, patching up the smoke-
pipe and chimney with some flattened out tins
and a bit of solder brought for the job. He fixed
up a bit of a bed, knocked a table up from old
boxes, brought in a paraffin lamp which he found,

good as new, on the dump. Arp made it into a regular home, and when the Old Cock looked by for his rent that first week he had to admit, "You made a regular home of it, Arp, you poor bombed-out sod. I reckon you've put the value of the property right up, a credit to the war effort. Good luck to you, Arp."

He was a lonely old cock, but that night he came in and they drank tea which Arp had brewed up in a big clean can, and the Old Cock split his cheese and raw onion sandwiches, two inches thick they were, and plenty for two. "The raw onion is the stuff," said the Old Cock. " Fights off the arthritis which is the curse of the country, Arp, keeps you regular and gasses the tape-worm. Not like the gas attack we done on the Cambrin front when me and old Taffy was watching it rolling over the shell-holes punishing the rats fat as porkers one early morning. The wind turned just when our bit of breakfast was ready, because we old soldiers reckoned you might as well get your lot on a full stomach, when back it come full pelt turning our badges, buttons, bacon, tea and all bright green as grass. That's when me stomach trouble started, a proper balls-up, what with our own gas and the lousy ving blong the Froggies was flogging us. They give me a few snug days in the hospital but I felt so poorly it was no rest really. You certainly made a nice little place here, Arp." The Old Cock gave Arp a picture of the good old King and Queen to hang up, and chipped in a bag of rare sugar and his tea ration, his contribution to their tea fund, always a smack in the eye to the enemy. Kaiser or Hitler they can't beat tea.

That night as it turned out was the first air-raid for a week. About one the distant throbbing started, the night beating like a big black heart, then sirens wailing up and down, on and on, searchlights swinging and pointing, guns cracking, then the bombs, booming in sticks of three and four and five and six, nearer and nearer, the sky glowing orange and then red as the fires started and spread, the fire bells far-off, the wardens' whistles shrieking, ambulance bells ringing.

Arp, a beaten dog, shook on the floor, shivering with cold, eyes squinted with fear of the next bomb, then body poised to flinch as the iron splinters struck and stripped him to ribbons, his voice struggling to release itself in a blessed scream, his memory racing back, back, down a long clattering tunnel to the heaps of rubble where this world of his started.

That night a little bomb was dropped by a damaged raider onto the nearby allotments. In the early morning when the Old Cock found Arp he was on his knees searching in the broken bricks and earth. He had found nothing although he must have been at it for hours because his hands were bleeding. His eyes were large and blank and his lips were mumbling. Maybe he had talked in the course of the night although now he could as usual say nothing. When the Old Cock asked what the hell he was doing he didn't know.

"If you was an old soldier like me," said the Old Cock, "you would take your kip when you can and if the bloody bomb's got your moniker on it at least you won't die tired."

He took Arp back to the Nissen telling him as they slowly walked about the time Taffy bought a Blighty one in the thick part of the thigh. "They was shelling us with these big bastards we called Jack Johnsons because they give out a lot of black smoke, and Taffy was just saying we didn't ought to call 'em that because Jack Johnson was more or less on our side and why can't we think of a good black sausagy sort of name for the bleeders. So I was saying Black Kraut Pudden, Shwartz (German for black) Fartz, Kaiser Bill's Balls, and so on, when suddenly old Taff grunts and goes down on one knee in a puddle of blood, but even that, Arpie old chap, wasn't too bad because it's a very full-time job to kill a bloke right out, always excepting, of course, bad luck and direct hits."

The Old Cock put Arp in the sun by the Nissen door, and brewed up the last of their tea. "It's always the same in war," he grumbled, "the tea just won't last out. Last time I see old Taffy he was humping coal for the railway so you can tell he didn't come to much harm, though of course in this war everything is more efficient."

When the Old Cock brought his tea out to him, Arp was still shaking a bit, although now he could think again and what he thought was I am glad I forgot what I forgot, I am glad I forgot. I forgot it all and I'm glad.

2

BY THE TIME the Hitler war was over (all bar shouting) Arp wasn't at all badly set up for a man who doesn't know his name, place of birth, the date of the happy event, occupation of father, or much else that way. He didn't have a passport, a work permit, or an identity card. He didn't know who his aunt was, where he went to school, what kind of an intelligence rating he had, although the Old Cock reckoned it must be low otherwise he would never be a rubbish-picker. All Arp knew was there is the rubbish-dump world, and it is his job to tidy it up, there being nothing against him selling a few bits and pieces to Rambam to pay the Old Cock, plus tea, bread, marge, a chunk of mousetrap and a piece of bacon, and what more (given a weather-proof Nissen hut which was worth a fortune in its day) could anyone want?

The Old Cock himself seemed pretty satisfied with peace. "Of course, Arp," he said when the dustmen brought the glad news that our gallant allies were all met up in Berlin, "it's been a bit of a picnic for us back here behind the lines, even though we have had our problems it's not like plum-and-apple made out of I wouldn't like to say, though we reckoned in the trenches the Maconochie tin of meat and veg was a banquet in its own way, but most of the contractors who fed us should have had their money stuffed into a couple of kit-bags round their necks and chucked into the deepest hole in no-man's-land. But even so I don't doubt they would have tinned the poisoned water itself. I'm not sorry the rationing is keeping on now the peace is declared. Rationing stops you chucking your money about on luxuries, just like they say in the papers, and we don't want to do that now, do we, Arpie? That's not going to be our problem, is it, old chap?"

He looked out over the rubbish dump, cluttered with unsorted rubble from the extra business caused by the recent war. He sighed. "No, Arpie, that heap out there is our problem," he said. "Look at me," he ran on. "I got me old missus to visit when the urge takes me, with a few flowers, chrysanthemums for choice, she was fond of them, me daughter down in Croydon married to a fellow with a leg wound back from Wopland and clerking again, with two nippers who I see regular as clockwork every Christmas dinner, me tobacco, me little cabin to have a doss in, and me old chum and neighbour, poor old Arp. Yet all may be spoilt by that festering mess. Look at it!" he suddenly shouted. "It's nearly full up — it's bloody near full up."

For now that the war was over the problem of the peace, as anyone with half an eye could see, was looming up clear against the skyline of allotment huts and ruined Rome, heaped high as hills and reeking with dust and the rubble of who knows how many homes for when you break it down what is the house of somebody (like Arp, say) but bits and pieces in a small space between streets? And now this same old tombstone rubbish dump, already congested when war began was now swollen by the busy bombs to greater heights than any planning engineer could deem safe or sanitary.

But you might say, supposing this old rubbish dump was full-up, and supposing the council who understand and control such things decided out of its store of experience to close the said dump, is there not in the very problem the seeds of its solution? Make new dumps in the spaces left by the bombs theirselves. Take over the holes where the houses were and fill them with rubble. Oh, you could go on all night like a proper local council meeting debating the ways and means of solving a silly question like this, till "Why, gentlemen," asks Councillor Stirp, "are we wasting time on this tidgy little question when there are acres of reconstruction before us?" Why indeed?

"Only," replies the Old Cock to the unspoken question Arp might have asked if his mind hadn't been elsewhere, "only, Arpie, old fellow, that if they close this old dump down, then, Arpie, old mate, that will be the last we shall see of yours truly, the silly old sod who guards the sodding place. That's all, old boy, that's all."

Which was why the Old Cock was crusty as all hell with the dustmen.

"Bloody lot of huns," he said after they'd been in of a morning and tipped their loads. "It's not right, Arp, the way I try to keep the whole place properly arranged for the council so as to give

[17]

them the best service and make it last out a good
long time more by scientific tipping of the stuff
in the right places — not to mention, Arp, the
way you do a good day's work day after day
picking over the dumps, and I got to hand it to
you, Arp, you poor old fellow, you leave everything a lot tidier than you found it. It's a crying shame the way those huns tip their loads and
scarper without so much as a by your leave. They
got no consideration for all the thought goes into
it, Arp. *They* don't give a cold sausage how long
the dump lasts out so *I'm* not going to be unduly
miserable about it, Arp, but if the council don't
look into it soon, the whole bloody dump's going to be used up years before its proper time. No
use telling them beasts. 'Hop out of it, Old
Cock,' that's all they say, spitting all over the
dump in a filthy manner, and making a mockery
of all our efforts. I don't half tell 'em a thing or
two — well, you've heard me, haven't you, Arp,
the bloody air turns blue with it, but what difference does it make — none — you're a witness
to that if the council ever starts sorting me out
because they're getting a bit strict now peace is
broke out — you can testify in a court of law
on your solemn oath, Arp, it's all those bloody

bastard dustmen with their pig-in-clover ways, making a disgusting pig-sty of the place. If I told the inspector once, I told him a dozen times a year, once a month when he looks round I tell him, 'Mark my words, Mr. Bates, the dump is going to be ruined by these hit-and-miss, airy-fairy, lazy-bugger ways.' He should worry. He retires with a half pension. A half pension. He'll be knocking down two-pound-ten a week, and he owns his own house and garden. I'll be off now then, Arp, down to the allotment. I'll bring you back a big cabbage, there's one I kept me eye on should be just about ready now, so we might as well get the benefit of it. Cheero, Arp, then, poor old chap."

Then Arp got on with peeling a few potatoes which the Old Cock had whipped from the allotments, in which exercise the veteran would never let him help, saying Arp was a specialized trades-man in the rubbish-picking while the gardening was the Old Cock's look-out in which duty he didn't need any help yet from a younger fellow, except maybe in the winter when you had to look further for your veg. But *what* an eye the Old Cock had for a cabbage, which was just as well because with his affliction he ate cabbage for three of them (boiled with a couple of thick rashers).

"Honestly, Arp," the Old Cock said when they finished eating and he broke wind a couple of times, "that was a real victory and peace-time dig-in, I reckon. We're a fair old cook I reckon, Arp, we're a fair old team. I don't mind telling you, Arp, before you dropped in it was a dead thankless job, and bloody lonely, because you can't say a civil word to them lousy dustmen, and that mister inspector Bates hates me living lights. Being like all merchants who have it cushy, he is a proper column dodger. But damn it all, Arp, it's not just the one job I got to hold down, remember. There's the old studio as well which is falling to pieces but suppose I don't keep an eye on it you're going to have gypos and tramps and all sorts of low-down riff-raff tearing and flogging strips off the place. It's a big responsibility for a man with a parasite in his gut. Want to take a turn round with me before kipping down for the night?"

Arp was nearly remembering something again, his eyes blank as they looked way off down the tunnel.

"It's a bit nippy out, Arp, if you're coming,"

said the Old Cock, knotting his choker. "Better do up your jacket."

As Arp's fingers buttoned the carefully darned dark blue fatigue blouse with the faded golden A.R.P. label over the left breast pocket, the Old Cock scratched his head, then carefully pushed the scurf out so that it fell tidily just over the hut threshold.

"You want to look out for a new jacket, Arp. All that A.R.P.'s a thing of the past. Now we got a jolly old peaceful world again, Arpie, you want to forget all that."

He watched Arp's fingers pulling the blouse down, tightening the belt so as to feel smart and properly dressed. "I reckon I ought to fix you up with a new name now we are victorious," he said, pulling his moustache hairs and remembering how he had christened him before, a barmy dazed and dusty fellow, blank-eyed with a dropped mouth and hands shaking, down at Rambam's shop, just after the Roman Road caught a packet the night of the big raid and the gas-works (which was always an eyesore) went up in a sheet of flame half a mile high. For that night Arp's lot too had copped out. Better, they agreed, if Arp had bought it himself at the same time.

"Better by far," old Rambam agreed, "better to go with the rest, better walk off into the dark holding a friendly hand than be left here in a darker darkness, the left hand the only friend the right has left. Better agreed, it would be better, only it didn't turn out that way so what bladdy nonsense is it to talk about better if? Better if such didn't come, that's what's better. Everything else is worse. And that's how it is."

"Better go down into the mud your fingers in the wind-pipe of a hun than be like that," the Old Cock said after looking at Arp.

"Sure better, certainly better, of course better. But the whilst here is a man who the shock has sent a bit quiet, maybe even a bit nervy."

"He looks barmy to me, the poor bugger," said the Old Cock still looking. "He definitely looks round the bend. Shell-shock."

"Maybe so," replied Rambam, "but at least it's company for you and he should be able to give a hand round at the dump where anyway it's a bit quieter than here with the lousy air-raid sirens every ten minutes. He can pick over the rubbish for bottles and such which I can buy and this way he'll scratch a living and you can't say it won't help you out. So what do you say?"

"I got enough to do without looking after war victims," grumbled the Old Cock. "I'm a bloody war victim meself, unpensioned."

"You want him to fall into official hands they should put him in a home?" asked cunning Rambam, knowing the Old Cock's down on any and all officialdom.

"Any refugee from them bastards, Mr. Rambam, I was about to say," grunted the surly Old Cock, "if you'll be so kind as to give me half a bloody chance, is abso-bloody-lutely welcome to hide out with me. So gord bless the Duke of Argyll. Come on, shortie. This way. Just a minute. What do we call him? What's his name and number?"

The Old Cock studied the dumb man in his still-dusty A.R.P. uniform, with his vague eyes and his arms hanging heavy as a punch-drunk boxer.

"I'll call him Arp," he said after a long look. "It's convenient, comes easy to the lips, and after all that's what he's labelled."

When Arp, on the Saturday of that first week, brought a sack half-full of junk down to Rambam's shop, the master rag-and-bone man gave him a few tips about what to look out for.

Within a few weeks Arp had taken to it like a duck to water, the pride and joy of old Rambam's professional life.

"You should see the state and condition of some of the gear is brought into this establishment week after week in a terrible condition," he told Arp. "But they are the sufferers in the long run because if there is extra work, Mr. Arp, I put it to you as one business man to another, if I've got to lay out for labour plus materials for picking and cleaning the gear then it's only right the price to you as the seller of the goods to me has to come down a little. Not that the market hurts *you* this way, because your goods are so nice set out and fixed up you are an example to all and sundry among my clientele."

Rambam looked up brightly at Arp standing there smiling.

"It's a crying shame," he mumbled, looking down and away. "Take another florin, Mr. Arp, do me a personal favour and take it."

But Arp didn't. He just shook hands with Rambam, and then pushed his packing-box and pram-wheels hand-cart out of the shop, and back up the Roman Road, stopping on the way to buy from the shops (who understood when he

pointed) some golden shag, a couple of yesterday's loaves, and for a treat for the Old Cock
(miserable old boy) two large Spanish onions.

Arp was very fond of the Roman Road because it was cobbled which gave a more interesting sound to the cart than any of your asphalted
roads where you can't hear a thing hardly, only
a squeak, clank, squeak. On cobbles it was more
interesting, especially if there was the odd horse
and cart, which more than likely there was, going to or coming from the brewery, smelling
of hops and malt and horse-dung. Also an interesting feature was all alongside the Roman Road
a sleeper fence with behind it the railway with
different trains, steam and electric, departing
for various quarters with either goods or pas-
sengers, and you would be surprised the number
of children who waved to Arp just as if he could
speak. But the best thing of all in the Roman
Road was the very tidy demolition site at the
end, just before Arp turned away over the Flats
towards home. It was the tidiest job ever, that
site. Even the bricks had been counted off and
stacked up neatly to one side, and the rubble itself was all shovelled into a pit where grass and
weeds were covering it up because herbiage al-

ways did better over the rubble, and there were no untidy pieces of stairs still hanging about, and no lavatories or fireplaces just left hanging. The whole lot was shored up with a couple of big bolted props, and the fence around was in good condition except for the posters which Arp always picked off as far as possible when he passed that way.

Arp stopped his cart in the gutter, lodging the right wheel so that it couldn't roll, and walked over and stood by the fence to look for a while at the demolition site. He looked over it from top to bottom, in the corners, down the slight hills and up the narrow valleys, squinted over at the tall weeds, and searched through the sparse grass. There was nothing for him to do here. Nothing at all. Absolutely nothing.

Once a man with a small pig nose and thick glasses with steel rims smoking a brown-stained butt stopped beside him and looked over the fence. Arp's fingers were idly picking away at a poster for the Alhambra (*Les Nudes de Paree*) and the man said, "What's going on, mate?"

But Arp just walked away without looking at the man because there was nothing, absolutely nothing going on there any more. Then later he remembered he left his cart behind so he had to go back. The cart was there. It had been empty anyway so nothing was stolen, but there was nothing on the site, nothing at all, absolutely nothing.

So although Arp was always a bit upset in himself about the site, by the time he walked back, the whole four and a half mile, he was his old self again (only who was he?) all bright and ready to listen to the Old Cock who certainly knew where and who he was in the world.

Take Ancient Rome, for example. The Old Cock was favourite on Ancient Rome, and when the evenings grew warmer they sat in the grass beneath the leprous, stucco columns, the Old Cock cracking away about how the ancient Romans brought law and order to damn near everyone even if it meant killing them, dead or alive they finished up with central heating, baths in excess, siege-engines and little glass bottles to cry into, till Nero put a match to the whole caboodle one night while feeling a bit down-hearted, thus passed the bloody glory of the ancients, notwithstanding its magnificence at the time, it being generally admitted they was amongst the world's great soldiers.

"So it makes you think Arpie, old sport,"

sighed the Old Cock, rising creakily. "It makes me wonder why I bother with the sodding rubbish dump. Coming for a turn round with me?"

After a moment his eyes lost the blank look and Arp followed the Old Cock out into the fresh blue night air, Arp a small perky figure like an irregular soldier, and the Old Cock big and shambling, in a choker and greasy cloth cap, a bit of cabbage still on his bushy tobacco-stained moustache, walking slowly off into the plaster ruins, the Old Cock still talking and Arp still silent as the rubbish dump beyond.

3

It was a bit difficult because just on the morning when Mr. Bates the inspector would decide to come, the Old Cock was out back standing on top of the clinker dump shouting blue murder at the dustmen who were tipping a mixed load onto it regardless and without so much as a by his leave, great lumbering horny-handed baboons. And it wasn't as if the inspector was alone. He had a man with him with a big red face with a nose like the prow of a ship sticking right up in the air as if he owned the rubbish dump. He looked a bit old-fashioned when he heard the Old Cock carrying on, although from where they were standing you couldn't see either the dustmen or the Old Cock, just hear them shouting back at him and him shouting back at them. So the upshot was Mr. Bates the inspector came over walking quickly, pulling down determined like his peaked cap with the council badge on it, closely followed by red-face prow-nose in a fancy check suit cream with little spots of every colour in it. They was walking straight up to Arp before he could duck back behind Westminster Abbey or safer still into the Nissen.

The inspector had seen Arp round the place, of course, three or four times, but no one wanted him to go asking himself if Arp was actually living there, in the Nissen hut, for example, and then asking himself if Arp was paying the Old Cock (strictly off the record) for the privilege of so doing. What Mr. Bates didn't know wouldn't hurt him, but now he was talking straight to Arp, with the Old Cock way back shouting his head off effing and blinding the council employees and the council itself, while here right on top of Arp was the council's own inspector, Mr. Bates himself.

"What are you doing on council property, my man?" asked Mr. Bates uppishly showing off before the red-nose. "The watchman here has the rubbish tip as well in his charge, Mr. Corst, and we get the odd vagrant creeping in while backs are turned. But the place isn't in bad order, Mr.

Corst, as you'll see when we go over it. Answer up, my man," he went on, turning back to Arp.

"My time's valuable," contributed Mr. Corst through his important nose.

Arp started to turn away thinking that this put the lid on it, the cat is right out of the bag, the Old Cock will be livid, but Mr. Bates, his long thin moustache shaking, one or two of the hairs coming free from the wax-fixative, caught Arp by the collar of his blue jacket-blouse and held on tight, his bony fingers pulling sharp downward then upward, rozzer-style, so that Arp just did what he always did in such cases, he jabbed his finger up at the old gold A.R.P. over his heart.

"You'll see, Mr. Corst sir," the inspector said, "an example will be made. Only those officially so instructed may enter here, the rest being tres-passers within the meaning of the law, and this man — why don't you speak when you're spoken to, man? Surly, you see, Mr. Corst, fed up he's been caught out — speak up, man."

But Arp just went on pointing at the gold label. Sometimes it took longer than others, but he was used to that.

"Guard," shouted out Mr. Bates. "Here, guard, it's Mr. Bates. Guard — forward guard."

Meanwhile Mr. Corst didn't lose valuable time with Arp and Mr. Bates. He was pushing hard at a small door in the middle of the big door to the main studio. But Arp could have told him to save his valuable time, because it was locked.

One way and another it was just as well the Old Cock had the good sense to climb to the top of the clinker pile and look over to see who was calling. Soon as he did his head snapped back and he shouted, "Right with you, Mr. Bates, sir, on my way, sir, don't panic there, I'm coming, inspector."

Then he slid down this side of the clinker pile, shinned up the wire fence by means of a couple of footholes kicked for the purpose, and dropped down with hardly a scratch about ten yards away from Arp and Mr. Bates who were now joined by Mr. Corst himself. He having discovered that the door was locked was saying through his huge boko, "Can we please have a little action, inspector, my time's valuable."

All of which began to get slightly up Mr. Bates' smaller but quite important nose because it didn't make things look very good for him and the council, so he shouted at the Old Cock, "I come here slightly unexpected, and what do I find, you indulging in coarse jests with your friends on the rubbish tip, and a tramp wandering freely round this valuable property. What's your explanation?"

When the Old Cock pointed out that Arp was acting lance-night-watchman completely unpaid, who didn't answer when he was addressed by Mr. Bates for the simple reason he was dumb, the inspector said they'd have to go into all that back at the council offices with the rating officer.

"Meanwhile," he added, "I have with me Mr. Corst of Hundred Per Cent American Films Incorporated" (and a few more hairs unfixed theirselves at the very name), "a prospective tenant of the council, and if you'll bear with us," he went on sarkily, "Mr. Corst's time is valuable and he wants to see over the entire property. You'll see, Mr. Corst," he said, as they walked on, "the sound-proofing is in excellent order. Our own engineer reckoned it altogether a very highly valuable installation."

The Old Cock looked back towards Arp, who still stood there waiting to see how it was all going to turn out.

[33]

"Oh, get on clearing up the filthy mess them dustmen left, Arp," he shouted, "you silly old fool. He's very useful to me around the place, Mr. Bates," he continued. "If them dustmen don't pull their socks up that tip is going to be useless to man or beast. This way, gentlemen. If it's convenient we'll have a look at the big studio first, shall we? I pop over and see it two or three time a night, Mr. Bates," he lied, "it's wife and child to me."

Now that Mr. Corst, thought Arp, is a real gentleman, you can tell by the way his finger-nails are finished off, a beautiful job, not to mention the shoes with their solid crepe soles, bad for walking on the slippery slopes of rubbish but you could go anywhere else in a pair of that quality, also the hair oiled and with hardly any scurf on the collar of his tip-top tailoring, and lovely manners, the way he said all about his time and that, not forgetting that valuable brick-red face which plainly cost a fortune in double whiskies, and the car a dark blue Bentley the likes of you and I would be only too pleased to be run down by. And the way he looks through you, like his mind is far away off on higher things like stuffed chickens and champagne cider and a bit of fluff in the back of that blue old Bentley, the dark horse with his big old nose, bless him. Poor Old Cock, thought Arp, with his dirty manners and his greasy cap and his tape-worm which no one ever sees, and his breath stinking of onions, and his shag-stained moustache, shambling along in front of a gent like that, not to mention Mr. Bates, with his bony fingers and bony eyes and bony nose and bony behind like a serge-draped knife-rest, and his peaked cap and his solid gold badge denoting a half-pension official inspector of rubbish tips and rotting studios. Why did they have to sort out the poor Old Cock, the bastards? And remember, please, that Arp was never one for bad language, especially in front of ladies, even thinking it that is.

"Bastards," Arp tried to say. He sat down by the weedy path. "Arrh" was all that came out even when he pressed very hard. "Arrh." Then when his lips came back together, "Pp," with a little plop.

After putting his tongue out, kicking a clump of grass to death, and blowing his nose with his fingers (a habit he detested) Arp went round to the rubbish dump to see what damage the dust-men had done. Just to show that he was on his home ground regardless of anything Mr. Bloody Bates might say (there he went again but that kind of bossiness always brought out the worst in him) he shinned over the wire fence by the special holes.

What a sorry sight met him on the other side of the clinker pile. Its whole lower end had been messed up by a load of miscellaneous which was nice pickings for him, but think of the Old Cock's dismay. Arp took out of his pocket the collapsible brass toasting fork which was his prodder, and started to pick away; and one in the eye for you Mr. Corstsir and Mr. Batessir. First thing that came to light was a battered Britannia metal cruet stand the like of which in all his experience Arp had never found, worth a florin of Rambam's money any Saturday of the rainiest month you like. Half of that definitely reserved for the Old Cock, in cash, added to the rent, let him treat himself whatever he fancied for his trouble.

Not that the Old Cock was being overworked, apart from the wear and tear on his boots from walking around, that is. Mr. Corst and the inspector climbed about the walls like a couple of flies, a thin blue one and a fat white one, dropping a few words like eggs and taking precious little notice of the Old Cock. Even so they kept him away for more than an hour, though credit where credit is due, when they left Mr. Corst slipped him two half-crowns practically under Mr. Bates' bony nose. Then they drove off in the big blue Bentley, Mr. Bates trembling like a girl with excitement when he got in and sat down next to Mr. Corst, who held the wheel above all the polished wood and chrome which shined and glistened like the mighty organ at the Granada Tooting coming up in the blaze of light from Mr. Bates' white envious eyes.

"And I wasn't sorry to see the back of the pair of 'em, Arp," said the Old Cock when he joined him again round by the dump. "That's a nice lot of pickings you got there, Arp. I like the cruet stand — never saw one of them dumped away before. But straight, Arp, I can't get down to it now, that Bates give me such a turn, that bloody tape-worm's killing me with its munch munch munch. I was awake the whole night listening to it. I done me best to think of it as a friend, Arp, really I have. But it's got no soul, Arp, not like you or I, it's just a blind groping worm without sense nor feeling, just a mad hunger, and then on top of that Bates has to sort me out, though that Mr. Corst is a right toff (did you see that car?), two half-crowns he give me, but I'm fair knocked out, Arp, you'll have to carry on on your own, I'm going to take a little nap if this parasite will leave me in peace, though I could have a bite to eat to shut him up, I suppose. I tremble to think how my stomach looks inside, Arp, honest I do."

When Arp looked in on him in his creosoted little hut at dinner-time he was sleeping like a baby, puffing out great clouds of onion and farting happy as a dray-horse. Arp waited for a few minutes to see if the worm would show himself like the Old Cock always swore they did once their victim was fast asleep through the open mouth of the defenceless sleeper. But there wasn't a sign of anything other than the Old Cock's great gobbler hanging down like a handful of giblets waving slightly in the oniony breeze.

Arp covered him up with his thin dung-coloured army blanket, and the Old Cock twitched like a dog and said "Yessir," then woke up, his eyes suddenly wide apart, frightened. "Did you see him, Arp?" he asked in a hoarse voice as if he'd been shouting in his sleep. "Did you see anything?"

Arp shook his head, but smiled to mean better luck next time. The Old Cock sat up with a moan.

"If we could only tempt him out," he said. "It might change me whole future."

He looked very old with the lines round his eyes, and the two deep lines down from the corners of his mouth, and the white bristles on the loose grey skin of his flabby jowls, and the old grimed knuckly hands rubbing themselves slowly together.

"Me stomach's fair caving in," he said. "What about a spot of din-din for a couple of good boys?"

He didn't mention their distinguished visitors again till that night sitting on the powdery crumbling steps of Ancient Rome.

"Mr. Corst reckoned Ancient Rome had a bit of life left in it yet," he said. "Well, look at it yourself, Arp, being practical for a minute — you've got your nice bit of horse-shoe seating over there with Old Vienna stuck in front of it but no trouble at all to shift, and perfect for the odd chariot race or chucking a few Christians to a few lions if you box clever and spread a couple of hundredweight of sand around first. Not to mention the steps on which we are now seated and on which them columns back there was formerly mounted in majestic splendour, nothing less, with that great triangle thing over the top. Cost a small fortune to build, Arp, let's be fair about it. And where better for the death of Caesar say, or Antonio's speech, or Rollmeover and Juliette me again — but joking apart, given a few good columns like this you can do the whole of Shakespeare, the whole lot, says Mr. Corst, and you know, Arp, I wouldn't put it past him, because there's a fellow really knows his onions. He gave me a dollar when he left you know, a dollar English not American of course which is naturally worth more than ours nowadays, Arp, although formerly of course the gold pound ruled the world. Ickabod, Ickabod, as the old preacher (what was his name) down at our chapel when I was a nipper used to say. And then with a wash and brush-up Baghdad can be quite resplendent, Arp, and that gives you the entire *Arabian Nights,* nearly a thousand stories, Mr. Corst says, entirely at your disposition, not to mention what I could tell him about the Messpot. Stink — it would stink your head off, Arp, and flies, you couldn't open your mouth without making a meal of them. But stretching from pole to pole is your unconquerable soul, Arp, so you get used to it, though you'd give your eye-teeth and balls for a cold glass of beer. Still that's life, Arp, as a gentleman like Mr. Corst knows, because he's been all over making films you know, from China to Peruvia and back. I'm going to get us a couple of bottles of bottled beer with that fiver he give me — no, Arp — I insist. The way that bloody Bates was shouting you about, manners of a pig, the dirty great yard dog."

The Old Cock had his mouth clamped down tight and sulky by the time they got back to the Nissen. He picked up his tin mug and chucked the cold slops clean across the room out of the door, though some fell inside.

Arp picked up his little shovel with a rust hole in it, and his worn-out but serviceable broom, and cleaned up the tea-leaves.

The Old Cock stepped over him bent down in the doorway, swearing as he passed. He took a few steps, head bowed forward, then swung round suddenly livid.

"Redundant, Arp," he said, "me redundant, meaning knackered, re-sodding-dun-sodding-dant."

He came forward, his eyes appealing, and caught Arp by the shoulder, pleading, "Didn't I tell Bates a hundred times, Arp, the dump will be filled up before it's time if they didn't get their rotten dustmen under control? Aren't you a witness to that, Arp? Cross your heart and hope to die, cross my heart and hope to flake out a pauper in the dirtiest ditch any mongrel-hound ever rolled over and pegged in. I told him, Arp — I told him again today. It'll get full up, Mr. Bates sir, I says, and then I suppose, I says, the council will have the trouble and expense of shifting me somewhere, and I'm the last one that wants to give the council any trouble, after all they been highly considerate of me, Mr. Bates, sir. 'You're getting past it, grown old and hateful,' he says. Me — getting past it. 'Another couple of months is all the tip's got left in it, and you about the same. You'll both be on the redundant stakes,' he says. Redundant. Him with his own house and garden and a fat half-pay pension to fall back on. I don't get a pension you know, Arp — only the regular old age."

The Old Cock's barmy old voice was quiet and cracky now, and Arp thought he certainly wouldn't take his beer from him. He filled up his mug with the cold tea and sloshed a good dollop of sugar and condensed milk into it and stirred it all up ready and gave it to the Old Cock.

"Tastes like boot-leather," he said, then seeing Arp's disappointed face, "Arp good boy, it's nothing personal to you, my dear. The most delicious tea would this minute turn a sour acid in me sickened tripes. The stomach is a weakly vessel, Arp, just now it turns and writhes with all its contents, those living, them consumed, and that not yet ejected in a regular manly way, the whole bleeding lot rears aloft accusing, throwing up heart and all at the rottenness of human kind, how unkind, how unhuman, its filthy face offensive to me low as I am fallen down to, yet I will die on this black spot of shame did I not hold meself the weeniest shade better than those weasels with men's faces who ignorantly shove their greedy snouts with fatal consequence into the vitals of any living creature handy, digging a grave in our misery. I am sick of the stink of the foul swine, Arp, that's all, the tea is a mere coincidence, it is not the disease itself."

He looked up at Arp, his eyes very bright with the fever of his sudden vision, his lips drawn back and open over the five blackish front teeth.

"What is man, Arp? Ask yourself the simple question, what keeps him alive? Forget for the moment boasts of bedizened piss-proud fools who call him god, lord of creation, or plain king of the animal world. Forget he is a masterpiece of the mastermind and all that crap. Look him bald in his damned face and see the thought working there of who can I catch and cook and eat, who can I suck dry as a fly, who can I stab for a fountain of blood to wash me paws in, who flog, who flay, who drive to suicide, who push to murder, who make quite useless, who curse redundant. For Bates hates me, Arp, as Cain hated Abel, and yet damn it, we are brothers and could surely have work together, sharing the loot gained from the rubbish dump as you and me do, Arp, but then I am a wrecked old cock, and you are what you silently are, and he is a fellow who believes in stepping-stones to the future, screw you, Jack, I'm alright, competition is the soul of success, success is the spur, it's just unfortunate if the spur happens to be in this case up our arse. He who will succeed must learn to enjoy the taste of

[44   ]

human flesh, Arp, for he is a cannibal and must live on others. I can't taste too good even with a few onions, a scraggy old sewer-rat like me's no grub for a gent, yet in the trenches we ate the rats for two weeks once, we and the officers messing together." He wiped his eyes and nose.

"Gord knows what's going to happen to you, Arp, if I get the push," he said. He hawked and spat. "Gord alone knows," he said.

4

IT WAS a week after the visit from Mr. Bates and his wealthy friend that Arp took a trip out with the Old Cock, down to see if Rambam had a coat the Old Cock's size, his old one being completely done in by acid from a bottle which was half-full with paraffin. Still, that's how it is, you never know your luck, and it turned out to be acid and burnt the Old Cock's hand so that he upset the lot all over his black overcoat which even with the weather getting a bit brighter, was still essential for the nippy nights.

Actually it was less than a week after, because the distinguished guests came down on a Monday, which was the worst day for the dustmen, who were completely browned off with the dustbins from the week-end being so full the stuff spilled out all down their backs when they shouldered them over to their wonderful new dustcart in cream and orange which the council had kindly bought them. And the day Arp and the Old Cock toddled off to look over Rambam's old clothes was a Saturday afternoon, the Old Cock reckoning that the dump and the studio could just look after theirselves for a change, he and poor old Arp had earned the odd outing. So they went off before dinner because the Old Cock had his wage-packet to collect as per usual from the council office, but instead of coming back as per usual (he said) a nice piece of skate and a few chips with plenty of salt and vinegar, a couple of slices, and two nice cups of chervy would just do the trick for their dinners. And afterwards Rambam. And afterwards, who knows, let come what will, adventure-bound he and Arp will take it all in their stride finishing up a perfect day with just a couple at the boozer, then back to their little grey home in the west and a long lay-in on the Sunday morning.

Those council offices fair knocked your eye out, having genuine marble walls and black-and-white tiled floors and polished wood doors and a bench with real cow-hide leather cushioning for Arp to be comfortable on waiting for the Old

Cock to complete his business and then, hey-ho for the bright lights. "Keep off the whisky and women, Arp," warned the Old Cock, "take a leaf out of my book and stick to beer, let others cop the scleroses of the liver and the King's bane, we'll be satisfied with a couple of pints. I won't be long, Arp, so don't wander around."

So Arp sat and waited hoping no one was going to be so stupid as to talk to him, and looking away (safety first) any time anyone looked as if they were about to throw even the mildest glance in his direction. Although the only real danger was from the hall-porter who from the back you might think was Mr. Bates in person, having the same distinct hatchet look to his shoulders, backbone and rump, though when he turned his noble ex-noncomm's face there was no moustache under a big soft red honest beer-drinker's strawberry nose.

It really was good having the Old Cock to go out with because he knew all sorts of stuff that Arp nearly remembered, like the Memorial Hospital is to our right, and that over there celebrates Nurse Cavell, and to our left is the children's playground, note the fine bust of Alderman Jakes by the gate, the pigeons shit on it only because they don't know any better, gord rest his poor soul he was the Old Cock's mate for a week years back when they worked the trams together, the Old Cock being driver for a time in his checkered career, but old Jakes was even then secretary of the union and he didn't half make a packet out of the pirate buses before the council took over buses and trams and showed an honest loss running them. Then on the compensation he goes straight, finishing up an alderman if you please, with a bust of his own.

The Old Cock remembered everything, even such things as the colour the old trams used to be before the council took over with the official cream and orange. And for Arp it was all useful stuff because it all reminded him, although of what he couldn't quite make out just now.

He sat for a while waiting, then got up to go to the gents after the long walk, seeing the sign just down the corridor ahead. While he was there he might as well have a wash and brush up, it being one of those pull-down towels all clean and fresh, and the liquid soap better than they used at home (you expect the best in a marble council office). He gave his fingernails a jolly good scrub, washed his face and neck, rubbed out his hanky and his shirt, nodding like he belonged there to a couple of workmen who popped in for a jimmy-riddle.

One of them said, "Getting stuck into it, ain't you, mate."

"Make yourself at home, cocker," said the other. "It's the only thing they give away in this joint. So like I was saying," he went on to his mate, "he reckons they was sitting with three face cards, three on the trot and him (according to him) with a prile of priles. Well, I say he's a bleeding liar. Have you ever seen it?"

"Never," replied the other doing up his flies.

"And I don't think you never will either," says the first. "After someone gives me that kind of bull you don't want to know, do you? You lodging here, chum?" he asked Arp. "Watch out the mayor don't cop you. So that's the last time I play cards with old Pudden Marshall," he said as they went out.

Arp gave them a shrug and a big smile as if to say I could tell you a thing or two if only I wasn't busy having a good wash just now. After they left he thought he might as well go the whole hog while he was there.

When the Old Cock arrived Arp was locked in the lavatory.

"Arp," shouted the Old Cock, "are you in there, Arp?"

Then he must have stood up on the wash bowl and lifted himself up to look over the top because suddenly his head on its tortoise neck peered over beside the cistern and he grunted, "I told you not to wander off, Arp, silly sod, didn't I? Put your shirt back on and get a move on do."

"That was very wrong of you, Arp," said the Old Cock, when they were back on the street, "to make yourself free with the council property. I always whip a toilet roll whenever I come down here but being a council employee it's fair game for me, still we'll overlook it this time."

He tore open his wage packet.

"Three pound six after deductions for health and that. I'm not doing too bad, you know, Arp, remembering it costs me nothing for lodgings. Post Office next to put away me nest-egg before the temptation to go good-time Charlie and blue the lot on riotous living. Or if you prefer we could make an early meal."

The Marine Fish Bar, plate lunches and suppers

served, was a bit of a let-down, there being only hot roe frying from midday, and no skate, plaice, rock-salmon, or even so much as a haddock fillet. But they had the potato scallops instead of straight chips, which made it up a bit, the lovely crisp batter done a treat on the slices of nice soft hot floury vinegar-soaked spud. The Old Cock's mouth watered right past his teeth and a few bits of warm hot roe landed right on Arp's hand when he said, "More *vinaigre*, parleyvoo for vinegar, Arp, take a liberal amount — and more bread if you want it, make a good meal, my treat, have some more chervy — two more cups, missus, and let your wicked old hand slip with the sugar. Live like fighting cocks, eh, Arp, like bloody bantams, let tomorrow come when it will, rain or shine, sufficient today is the evil therefrom and the devil take the hindermost. Two more scallops, missus, and four pennorth of chips. Get stuck in, mate."

Arp fidgeted his shoulders to shift the still wet shirt, and got stuck in.

As they chumped contented, a little nipper with a runny nose kept saying, craning his neck back to look up to the top of the high newspaper-stacked counter, "A sixpenny lump and three pennorth, missus, a sixpenny lump and three pen-north, missus."

The Old Cock, full of beans from the gorgeous lashings of crisp golden fried chips, scallops and hot roe leapt up from his brown bent-wood chair and picked up the nipper by the elbows, holding him high above the counter.

"Now tell the lady, Tiny," he cackled, "look at this, Arp — all done by careful leverage on the elbows. Oh me back," he said suddenly, letting the boy jump down. "I forgot me old back-wound, Arp. That rotten hun shell I copped at Wipers still pays me out alarming. Eat up your scallop, Arp, I'll be alright."

He stuffed five succulent soft chips together into his aching gob, singing.

"By ob ba a baba," sang the Old Cock as he swallowed the chips.

> *"My old man's a dustman*
> *One poor fellow with a bullet up his arse*
> *He fought in the battle of Mons,*
> *Killed five thousand Germans*
> *With only fifty bombs.*
> *One lay here,*
> *One lay there,*
> *One lay round the corner,*
> *Was crying out for water,*

Water, water come at last,
A fly come along and pissed —"

"None of that, I say none of that, if you please," said the missus. "An old man like you ought to be ashamed to carry on so. There you are, sonny," she went on, handing the nipper his six-penny lump and three pennorth. "And that'll do from you, sir, if you don't mind."

The Old Cock was a bit put down at that.

"Old gallant old honourable old fighting song," he mumbled to Arp, his cunning old eyes squinting over to see where she was. "Old contemptibles old marching song, Arp," he mumbled, nibbling a scallop, a large portion of batter-case dropping down on to the floor. "I done me duty for King and Country, got trench-fever, dysentery, malarial in the Messpot, and a great thumping lump of shell shrapnel half-way up me backside, only to be told to stow it by a madam in a fish-and-chip shop. Carry on grub-bashing, Arp — ignore the mannerless old cow."

After dinner, since Rambam's was only round the corner, they went down there to see about the new second-hand coat for the Old Cock.

"We want to be very nice to poor old Rambam," said the Old Cock. "Remember, Arp, it

[54   ]

was him who put me on to you as a good candidate for permanent picker on my dump, and many a good pint of wallop I've had against his reckoning, a couple of bob here for this and a couple of bob there for that, all goes to make the world go round, Arp. And fair's fair, he done me a very good stroke indeed when he put me on to you, Arp, old fellow, and you likewise, you could have been wandering round the dustbins wasting your efforts on the pennies when you could be in the shillings by working at the source, which is my old rubbish dump. Remember, Arp?"

And the funny thing was that Arp could remember all that, every detail clear as a gin optic, starting with walking out this end of the long clattering tunnel, looking out over the dumps, then knowing it was up to him to tidy up a bit, and after that never looking back (couldn't if he wanted to) but pick-picking away with his hands (that was before he found his brass collapsible picker) in the dustbins and little local rubbish piles.

"You might be wandering around, Arp, a casual," said the Old Cock rolling himself a shag cigarette. "No place of your own but sleeping round the bomb-sites in the old shelters with the deep puddles, those that aren't completely flooded that is, which is no joke once the weather breaks after the summer, with the courting couples chucking you out of the really dry shelters where you could have a decent kip while they waste your chances with their give-over-do-Alfie, while Alf just as you might expect, slips his hand up a bit further and breathes hard down the front of her dress. Not to mention rats. Not to mention the stinking tom-cats. Not to mention fleas which you can't see how they live on in the empty shelters but they do alright. Not to mention the rozzers always on the prowl, and the nippers exploring for hidden treasure, an old rusty can of onion soup or a rotting gas-mask or a french letter which has had its day."

The Old Cock sadly mopped up his vinegar with a bit of soft bread and fed it into his slobbery old face past its five black tomb-stones. Arp still had a scallop left. Nobody but nobody had Arp's luck, especially now that the shirt was pretty dry on his back, and the great splendid dinner warm in his tum, lucky old Arp.

"It can be cruel lonely up there on the heap," the Old Cock rambled on as they continued their promenade. "Sometimes, Arp, I used to sit in me little dark brown hut with the paraffin lamp smoking away smudging and stinking the place up. The tortoise stove was cold, and the plate from me dinner thick white with fat and yellow with a smear of egg, and the chervy cold in the pot, and the photograph of me missus looking accusing-like. I thought of me daughter and her celluloid-necked old man clerking his guts out poor but respectable as a bank-manager with his long white nose going waxier every day, and me two grandchildren, Hilda, age three, and Lawrence, age five, who I see last Christmas with a bunny rabbit for her and a plastic machine-gun for him, and gord blimey, Arp, I fair puked me heart out. A man fights his life out for his family, Arp, and at the finish what has he got? A stuck-up daughter too good to care whether he's croaked between Christmas dinners, two lovely grand-nippers going their way with a bunny and a machine-gun into this wicked world of care and strife, and nothing to call his own except a steaming rubbish-tip and a munching tape-worm. And I'm a chap, Arp, who likes a bit of company and a spot of chin-wag. Here we are at Maison Rambam, a square deal for the boys of the rubbish brigade — where are you, Arp?"

Arp was standing up the Roman Road down which they had just walked, or rather the Old Cock had walked talking away a hundred to the dozen, never noticing the demolition site so tidy that Arp felt he had to look over just once again, and maybe pick a bit more poster off the fence. How did they ever get the bricks with their broken corners so tidy as that?

"Gord stone the crows, Arp," puffed the Old Cock, coming back, "what are you looking at, cock? There's old Rambam waiting for us and you sky-larking around like a five-year-old. Don't look so miserable, Arp, old chap, you can't expect to find something in every pile of junk. My hat, what a jolly good job the demolition boys made of that lot. You got to hand it to that thieving band of brothers. They certainly can tidy a place up so it's a fair treat to gaze upon. Come on, sonny, Rambam's waiting."

And he put his arm through Arp's pocketed arm and led him off away from the tidiest site in the world.

"You're a teeny bit naughty today, Arp, aren't you," he said. "You're in one of your moods, I could tell when you disappeared down at the council building. Here we are then, clean, bright and slightly oiled, bargain-hunting for a capote, a cloak, a reach-me-down, a top-coat, a nice heavy overcoat not to exceed the enormous price of half-a-bar, ten silver shillings, five florins if you care to put it that way. What can you offer a gent in the council service?"

"I'll put a few fairly suitable garments out for you to inspect in your own time," said Rambam, bobbing about with his darty eyes dark as damsons and his mouth smiling away over lots of white teeth not his own and a bit loose.

"You're looking well, Mr. Arp," he said. "He's a real tidy sort of fellow, Mr. Arp is, isn't he, guvner? I always tell some of them when they complain, if they brought in the goods as spick and spanking tidy as Mr. Arp does, they wouldn't have nothing to complain about, though doubtless they will still complain, mankind being what the Almighty in His strange way has seen fit to make him. Yes," he went on, lighting up a flat brown scenty sort of cigarette, "yes indeed, Mr. Arp, you are certainly coming on well since you took up with the guvner here. I bet he's a credit to you, isn't he, guvner?"

"I don't much care for the black one," said the Old Cock, taking it off, "alright for an undertaker's mute or a sanitary inspector who isn't likely to go redundant come the summer, but not for the likes of an old infantry-man like me."

"Try the nigger brown," suggested Rambam. "That redundant is a horrible word. It stands for fired, sacked, chucked out, don't it?"

"Never mind all that, Rambam," said the Old Cock a bit angry, "the coat I got a fancy for is right here," and he tugged away at the corner of the coat rack. "Right, right here," he grunted, pulling out a fine grey coat, with a special black cotton covering over it to keep the dust off.

"Not that one," said Rambam quickly, "if you don't mind, guvner, that one is not on the market just now."

"Condition of sale, Misterambam," said the Old Cock, "none of your lousy old condition of sales. I want the grey and I can pay. Tucking it away for some rotten clerk in the bloody council building, I suppose. They think they own the world, those pea-eyed pacifist arse-kissers, but they don't. How much for the coat?"

"Mr. Arp," said Rambam, standing in front of the coat, "just pop over the road for me, if it's not asking too much, and get me a box of Swan matches for fourpence. Here is the money."

[60   ]

As Arp stood at the shop-door the Old Cock was carrying on alarming. "Never mind changing the horse-thieving subject," he cracked away. "How much for the ropy old coat?"

"Please, please, guvner," pleaded Rambam, "one minute — Mr. Arp, straight across the road if you don't mind — just for a personal favour for me — that's right — I'm much obliged to you for your kindness. Now," he went on in a confidential voice after Arp was over the road, "be so good not to make a fuss but listen."

The Old Cock, sulking, threw the grey coat down on the floor, and Rambam picked it up and dusted it carefully like it was alive but rather weakly.

"The coat, my dear sir," he said, "this coat, please understand, is not for sale, for the simple reason it is the unclaimed property of that poor dumb creature, unfortunate man, the coat and one or two other remnants an old woman picked up and brought to me, after the catastrophe. You done the right thing and fixed him up at your place. You give him a new life. You want now the remembrance of the old should take away the joy from the new?"

"Oh gord," whispered the Old Cock. "Oh

Christ, oh gord, put it away quick and say no more, he's coming back. It's a mercy he's got no more sense than voice, poor nameless bastard. Excuse my rudeness, Misterambam. I'll take the brown coat."

"That will be seven-and-sixpence then," said Rambam. "Thank you, Mr. Arp, for the Swan matches. It's wonderful the way you get around in spite of your affliction, but fear nothing, Mr. Arp, there is a meaning in everything and everything has a meaning. It is not for us to question providence because even if we was to get answers for our trouble we are like ants on an ant-heap when a man is speaking — we would not understand the meaning of those very answers. So who wants to speak, so long as you have your health and strength, a bite to eat, a friend to eat it with, and a dry, clean place to lay down to sleep. Take the coat for seven-and-six, guvner, and go in health the pair of you."

"We'll be off then," said the Old Cock, "like me new coat, Arp, old horse? We got all our shopping to do remember before the boozers open, then one for the road and home, Arp, Pip-pip, Misterambam. Come on, Arpie."

But Arp was watching how tidy Rambam

folded the arms of the grey coat together over the breast like the coat was praying, then turned the skirts up carefully, smoothing the folds out, then wrapped the black cotton remnant round it and put it high up on a shelf on one side like a very special job waiting. Which you could see it was, though for who? A pity it didn't have a label on it which would have helped. A grey coat with a black lining. Arp wondered if there was a small burn on the right sleeve. Then he wondered why he wondered. Why? he wondered. Who?

5

I<small>T WASN'T</small> an old farm-cart overloaded with ma-
nure and creaking. It wasn't an old horse wheezing. It wasn't an elderly spinning jenny spinning,
or a ghostie groaning, or a speaking pig grunting,
or a sparrow croaking. It was the Old Cock singing through the dark with Arp trotting away in
a little jig beside him, holding on like grim death
to his sinewy venerable arm to save him sinking
on his ancient withers in the mucky gutter.

> *"Oi bainted 'er*
> *Oi bainted 'er*
> *Darn ve belly an up ve back*
> *In evverry ole and evverry crack."*

"Not that I could nowadays. I'm past it now,
Arpie, redundant now, old boy," he blathered
boozily, "but mark my words, Arpie, mark 'em
careful now because I'm not a boasting man and I

[64]

won't never say this to you again, I have been through the lot in my time, Arpie, and it's not worth a light. Oh yes, when your backside's polishing the top-sheet and you're coming round Tattenham Corner into the straight, provided she don't suddenly say like mine used to, I see Sainsbury's have got ginger-nuts in their window this week I think we'll have some of them, certainly when you're standing proud, Arp, and your lady fair is giving you a bit of respect, then I admit it makes the world the bloody world go round. And as for do without it, Arp, I seen boys of nineteen and twenty stand on a queue on short leave from the trenches chafing like horses and just as patient so long as they know their turn at the trough is coming up before the next bombardment takes their bull virginities to where there's no grave for 'em. Take it from me, I seen the lot — the lot, Arpie. I seen all shapes and sizes in many different disguises and it's the same perishing thing afterwards, whether you have red-head or yellow hair or brown, black or common house mouse-colour, all except my poor Martha and she's passed over gord rest her suffering soul. She was an angel, Arpie, nothing else but an angel, gord bless her dear red-rimmed eyes because she was the blood-

[65]

iest woman for crying I ever knew all my rollicking life. Dear weepy potato-faced Martha, the best wife gord ever sent a human man."

He shook himself free of Arp's detaining hand and tripped face first on the slippery stone kerb, then sat up, pulled his cap off, and wiped the blood away from his snotty battered nose.

"Don't panic, Arp, poor chap," he slurred. "It's no more than I deserve. This blood will be sacred to the memory of the dearest companion mortal yet has known."

He pulled himself up by Arp's wrists and stood groggily leaning up against a lamp-post, the light making the blood black as it regularly ran down his chin on to his disarranged choker.

"I'm a lousy useless old rotter, Arpie," he whispered, fat tears edging greasily between the hairs on his cheeks.

Arp got out his clean hanky, still a bit damp, and wiped the Old Cock's face, but it was only first aid and he remained a mess.

"That was quite a clonk I clocked up there," he said, opening his rheumy eyes, "but a spot of blood-letting is healthy and takes off the alcaholickel fumes from the nut. Seven, no eight pints I took, Arpie boy, no nine. I got to have a slash or bust."

He stumbled to the wall, lurched along holding it with his finger-tips and disappeared between two iron gates, a black mouth into the dark.

Arp sat down and pressed his stomach, full up and lap-lapping with two and a half chill floating pints of pig's ear, both mild and bitter, a brown and a milk stout. His head was still playing on the jangly battered joanna in the Bunch of Grapes where everything had been so jolly old pals. He pressed harder with flat hands. Apart from a cold sausage each they hadn't eaten a thing since dinner. Arp's stomach felt cold and all awash, and a bit of milk stout kept coming to the top and then diving down again into his guts. He wished he was in bed tucked under a nice warm one. A nice warm coat. With a little burn in the sleeve. Arp stood up. There it was again, the little mouse memory. Now it was gone and the Old Cock was calling him.

"Come here, Arp, for Christ's sake, Arp, come here."

He was striking matches and peering down through the dark at the ground. As Arp stumbled through the gates, turning towards the flickering matchlight, the Old Cock started to call quite loudly in a blubbery voice, "It's a judgment, a judgment. Martha, forgive me, forgive me, Martha. I never meant no harm to a hair of your head even if I did give you the odd slosh in the kisser, you always give back as good as you got. I'll never touch the booze again, Martha, it's the booze makes me mad, that and throwing a bloody pick and shovel day after day. Forgive me, Martha."

When Arp had scrambled across the headstoneless graves, kicking over a jam-jar with a few wet stalks sticking in his sock, to where the Old Cock lay crying his eyes out on the grave of his passed-over missus, he looked up heart-broken.

"I made water on her grave, Arp," he said. "I made water on her lovely innocent grave. That stone's solid Ferrara marble, Arp, I give her a good sending off with the son-in-law's help, the mean bastard, like getting gravy out of a dried turnip. Look at the inscription," he went on, kneeling up to strike a match. "A perfect wife, a perfect mother, and a perfect soul, Martha, wife of — "

He stopped, focusing his eyes on the words.

The match burnt down to his fingers and he dropped it.

"Hold on, Arp, hold on, not so fast, let's take another look here, I suspect jiggerypokery and skullduggery, let's have a proper look."

He struck another match and bent close to the stone, his eyes squinting over word after word.

"They've displaced her, the poor redundant cow," he said, his breath bated with shock. "This one says Frederick Pile, age eighty-two, they've thrown my Martha out for a mess of pottage. I'll see something is done about this, Arp," he said, "follow me, Arp," and he tripped over the graves (though never actually hitting ground again) back to the grave-yard gates. There he looked up at the gates, and shook his shaky fist.

"Revenge," he shouted. "Revenge on the Manor Forest Cemetery. Just a minute."

He squinted up at the sign, then went on in a suddenly sobered voice, "Technical error, Arp. It's the wrong cemetery. The district's lousy in 'em."

The Old Cock wiped his eyes on his elbows, his nose on his cuffs, his mouth with his hand, and rocked off up the road singing at the wavering top of his off-key voice.

[69]

"Oi bainted 'er
Oi bainted 'er
Darn 'er Droory Lane
Oi bainted 'er ol tomarrer
Overa overa gayn."

He stopped suddenly and turned.

"Gord's truth," he said with a beery gust of shock, "I forgot to pop me nest-egg in the Post Office and now we gone and blued the lot but for," he raked out his trouser-pocket with a shaking hand, "one pound note and eight shillings and two tanners and one joey old type and one joey new type which I think is the daftest-looking coin ever minted and four-five-sevenpence-halfpenny in copper. You look after the pound note, Arp, for safekeeping, it's not safe in the burning pocket of a low-living knockabout like me. Forward into the valley of death marched the poor bloody infantry, forward march, Arp, and never look back, boots, boots, boots the boys are marching, cheerup comrades they will come, four and twenty pair of 'em, boots, boots, up and down and up again. You can't beat the good old songs of the PBI, Arp, it's Tommy this and Tommy that and Tommy sod off out of it, but it's what will you have, Mr. Atkins, when the guns begin, Arp.

Those minniewerfers whining right past your earole, I can hear 'em now."

So into the night marched the gallant pair, the Old Cock passing the time with singing, jigging, a clog dance, falling over, starting a fight with a telegraph pole, and once going silent for a short space to bring up under a sheltering wall, but quite soon talking again, and jigging, and talking and talking. So they came home about one in the morning, the Old Cock hoarse and faint with the walk and the beer and the puking and the talk, and Arp wishing he was in bed tucked up if possible in a nice grey blanket-coat.

When they came round the bend in the road on to the home stretch and, looking ahead, felt glad to see the looming lines of the empty studio behind which they could only hope the rubbish tip had possessed itself in patience through their long day off, they stopped dead as one tired man, looked again, and looked back to one another.

"It's all lit up like Crystal Palace. Pinch me, Arp," whispered the Old Cock, "pinch me hard, Arp, I'm going stone raving barmy here, the old wallop has reached me braincase and touched me off. Here, give us a good slap in the kisser, that'll bring me round."

He grabbed Arp's hand, made a missing slap at his face with it, then looked again.

"It's thieves in the night, Arp, prepare for offensive, peep-peep, over we go, on the bayonet. No. Let's box it clever and panther crawl to striking distance. We'll have to watch out for sentries."

He dropped to the ground and started to crawl jerkily forward, Arp following on hands and knees.

As they came up opposite the wide-open gates, keeping heads well down and bottoms up, what turned out to be a blue Bentley nearly ran them over, but stopped with screaming brakes and a smell of rubber.

"What the hell d'you guys think you're at?" shouted a voice, and, luck of the draw, it was their old benefactor with the valuable time, Mr. Corst, his honoured and revered self.

"Touch your forelock to him, Arp," muttered the Old Cock, "he's a walking gold-mine, many's the half-bar he's dropped me in the past. Mister Coarse," he said cheerily, "Mister Corsir, it's a privilege and a pleasure to see you again, sir, as soon as me and me old chum, Arp, get the bloody thieves out of the old pig-stysir, it's yours to climb over till kingdom come or you break your neck because them stairs is definitely not safe as I've often told Mr. Bates hisself, bless the old gentleman."

"Tell the burbling moron to stop yakking and make way," snorted Mr. Corst in a surprisingly unfriendly manner. And who should emerge from the car, his dark blue rain-coat spreading like bat's wings in a sudden puff of wind, his hatchet-head poised for a good hard chop, his winkling moustache cracking with static, but old house-owning, pension-winning, badge-flashing Bates himself, his quick old thin nose wrinkling away as he smelt (as who could not?) the booze-fume laden breeze billowing out from the Old Cock's wide-open frightened mouth.

"You've gone too far this time," he growled, the tyke. "Take him off out of it," he snapped at Arp, "get him out of the way."

Because what with the joy of seeing Mr. Corst and the fright of seeing you-know-who, the Old Cock had passed clean out.

So what with one thing and another it was hardly to be wondered at that the pair of them passed disturbed nights. The Old Cock's turnip watch said three-fourteen when he woke up croaking, "Where am I, where am I?" and found himself neatly stowed in the usual bunk with his blanket kicked off and his boots in a tidy pile below. He lit the lamp with a shaking hand, turned Martha's fly-blown faded-indigo contemptuous phizog to the wood wall, slipped his high brown stockinged feet into the boots, and limped out into the freshish pre-morning air, his bowels cleaving to his chest-bone and his mouth like a pet-shop floor. He heard a clatter and a clanging all about the place, lights everywhere and the odd shout, but the hell with it, he was too old for these larks, he should know better than to drink, it was the tape-worm's awaited opportunity and absolute murder it kicked up out of its beastly spite. He limped out to the nearest gents.

One thing they weren't short of around the place was gents, the entire studio being lavishly provided with several styles of WC, though his regular one was a ladies which he used not for immoral reasons but simply because it was the nearest and comfortable, no leaks in the roof. He settled himself down and thought how when you was truly old nothing went right for you. Nothing at all, no matter how it started out, ever worked out right in the end. He rubbed his nose carefully, then massaged it with the gentle fingers of both hands, easing it back into shape, and then systematically picking the bits of blood off wondering whether it would start bleeding again. Falling about like a clown in front of everybody. Everybody watching. Making a side-show of himself, a man with several medal ribbons and a former heavy-weight class boxer, can't hold his piddling drop of drink in front of everybody. Oh blind O'Reilly, he thought suddenly, standing up and hiking up his trousers (nothing accomplished, nothing done), *Bates*.

The Old Cock bustled out of the ladies shrugging himself fully awake, and taking great lungfuls of air. Supposing *he* was still about? What the Christmas was happening anyway? Lights, and all sorts of row, and the place lit up like Crystal Palace. He collected his acid-burnt coat, the new seven-and-sixpenny number being left gord knows where in the preceding frolics, and set out for the doors of the main studio where the clanging was most energetic. Workmen, knocking themselves up for the double-time money, were running around like fleas, banging this and sloshing distemper on that, and dragging poor old Ancient Rome through the big double doors now thrown wide open and cluttered with gear from a nearby lorry. But no (thank heaven) supervising Bates in sight, only a normal foreman knocking steaming tea back straight out of a tea-can.

"Mr. Corst about, mate?" asked the Old Cock, making it sound as if he knew the guv from years back at college.

"He's taking a kip down at the production office," said the foreman putting the can down after a last long draught and removing a butt from behind his ear. "He's got a sekketary and all that down there. Marvellous, how the poor live, ain't it? He carries a box of cigars and a pint of whisky wherever he goes. Marvellous, ain't it? Get your fingers out, boys," he shouted, "let's get it over with and go home."

With a bit of luck, the Old Cock thought, king-pin Bates will have gone by now, by bike for preference, with no rear lamp and (how sad) got himself run over by an all-night milk van.

"Take it careful with them columns," he said, as he went out, "they cost a fortune in their day."

"We're dead careful," answered one of the men, kicking a column so hard a lump of plaster jumped right off it. "What you left over from, mate, the wreck of the *Hesperus?* To you, Charlie," he went on, "I said to you, you berk, not from, to."

Peeping through the window of the production office the Old Cock saw that there indeed was Mr. Corst sleeping like one of Dr. Barnardo's innocent babes on a sofa, while in the next office a tired old horse-faced judy with her overcoat on was banging her fingers down to the knuckle typing. He nipped round to the door and poked his head in.

"Inform Mr. Corse that the night-watchman looked in on his regular second round of the property and begs to report that everything is going ahead as per plan. What's going on, miss, if you can spare a tick from your sekketarial labours?"

"A Mr. Bates was looking for you," she said, "if you're the watchman."

"Dear old Batesy," laughed the Old Cock, "old chum of mine for years. What a shame I missed him. Must have been making me round of the tip at the time. I got the two responsibilities, you understand, miss. If I'm not here, I'm there. Got no time to waste sleeping on this job unfortunately, though I can't be in both places at once, can I?

How was the old fellow? Didn't wait in the chilly air, I hope, not with his weak chest?"

"Mr. Corst and the inspector had to go back for the duplicate keys because you weren't to be found. The time they lost on the big studio and everything because of that."

"Thick as thieves those two, ain't they?" laughed the Old Cock, killing himself with enjoyment. "Did you hear we had a bit of trouble round the tip tonight? Burglars. I fought the lot off single-handed. You can't beat the old military training in an emergency."

"Don't tell me," said horse-face, "tell them." And went on typing as if her life depended on it, as in a way it did.

Miserably trying over a few old lies in his mind the Old Cock made his way round to Arp's Nissen and opened the door carefully.

"You awake, Arpie?" he inquired in a soft voice. "Awake, old man?"

Arp was, and glad to be, due to him having had that dream again, waking up with a headache from the clattering and darkness in the tunnel.

The Old Cock sighed as Arp swung off his bunk.

"Let's have a brew-up, Arpie, thanks be that

in our frolicking you didn't lose the grocery bag, faithful chum, so maybe a couple of rashers'll go down well. The worse has happened, Arp. Due to me being absent without leave when the brass-hats descended on us like the wolf from the fold, we are about to be chucked clean out of our snuggery. We have seen, Arpie, the best of our days, and now we got the dirty end to come. The huns are here."

6

ALL through the Sunday the workmen ding-
donged away getting the studio smarted up with
Mr. Corst keeping his eagle eye on things and Mr.
Bates making an exception which proved the rule
and coming in to work of a Sunday, his fresh
shirt for the Lord's Day gleaming unnaturally
against the unhealthy purple of his knobbly
adam's apple, resplendent with the seedy magnificence of his dark blue serge issue uniform, the
best one (it goes without saying) for a special
occasion like this when the pound notes were fly-
ing about like bluebottles round a dustbin on a
hot summer morning.

Oh a one-eyed sailor could see well enough that
Mr. Corst was the gift of heaven to any council
you like to name. Oh, what a gorgeous tax-
worthy gent of the old school with bells on, oh

what an appreciator of land-values, substantive captain of industry, employer of grateful labour, respected prospective citizen of the district and grand master of a local lodge, what an enviable whisky-sodden nasal nagger of nature into productive channels. Oh what a fortune in rates. Oh glory oh our island story, America we love thee especially thy valuable time-saving son-of-a-bitch (we know the lingo) ex-major of the special entertainments for doughboys division of the Army Air Marine Corps (pass the ammunition) Corst, unbeknownst to anybody (especially the poor bloody bedizened council) a virtual bankrupt trading on a distribution contract provided by the husband of an ex-wife (the best of good friends) lush with the unexpected success of his latest epic saga of this girl who. Good old conman Corst, out now to make a cheapie on the quickie in this wanky old barn the council is loopy enough to let him have for a nominal month's advance (better than letting it fall down from the rot, said Councillor Coldwell, and if he defaults we get it cleaned up for nowt). Hail Corst, a producer in production.

All credit to the man who first dreamed up credit, be his skin of whatever hue, generously thought Producer Corst, president of this, vice-president of that, chairman of a couple, and managing director of the lot, all of them not worth a fart without credit. Credit which maketh the whisky to start out of cold-water taps, the cigars to send off Indian-style smoke signalling the bean-feast is now on in a private suite at Claridges, or the Mount Royal, depending on the production budget, and Corst to stand up piss-proud as a king, his big red neon nose flaming out bravely to pull putrescent randy glances from everything in skirts (whichever way you like it, Mr. Corst) and nervous glad-to-kiss-your-royal-hundred-per-cent-gold bum smirks from the Bates of this council-planned world.

"But I don't give a monkey's if he's the biggest double-dyed villain and shitehawk between here and the Elephant and Castle," observed the Old Cock, "he'll be a mother to me and the Pope's bull so long as I don't lose me job. If I do, though, Arp, it goes without saying he is a low-down bastard not fit to clean out the latrine-pits, though pray gord the situation don't arise. Every time I see him I'm touching the old forelock like I got a tick, grinning away like a loony. The officer class expect it, Arp, and don't you forget it. Give at least a couple of salutes any time you should have the misfortune to run into him, thus making it clear you're killing yourself for the good old cause of squire Corst, bless the guvner. Bates is going to be on the look-out for me this afternoon. I can feel it in me writhing gut. If I don't get the bullet from one I can get it from the other. Let's toddle over to the good old friendly rubbish-dump. They shifted Baghdad and Westminster into the big studio today. I only hope they know a good thing when they see it, and treat them ruins with respect. Forward into the valley of death, Arpie, poor daft coot, let's get out of harm's way."

Meanwhile in his present inconvenient surroundings Mr. Corst was making the best of things, down to the last few cigars and the last half-case of scotch, grateful to providence for having provided a new company which could open credit accounts with suppliers who had not before had the pleasure and proud privilege to supply him with the necessities of life. Soon he would give a party, boy what a party, with performing seals maybe, and even a small elephant, a party with a circus theme, everybody please come as a circus thing, clowns and bareback riders a speciality, and him, of course, a ring master in red velvet with a whip, cracking away at one or two of the really big boys with the right kind of know-how and what-with to further the at-present slightly dipped future of Claygate Corst, who certainly knew how to put on a dandy and unusual and entirely darling party.

But for the time being, work. To work, Corst, get something moving, we got the backing, we got the brains, energy, and the credit, we got Roda Randolf, thirty-eight bust, hips powerful, waist minuscule, we got poor old dipso Maxie Fantano, a great in his day, three Oscars and four wives and stuffed full of liver inside from rich living; with a yellowing artistic licence to sell himself up the creek if there were still any buyers, which it so happened there weren't except for Corst. Dear charming old Maxie who laid anything that in his miasmal permanent drunk sounded in the far-off haze like a doxy, but a demon with the camera when sober, a name to conjure with (if there is still a public for conjuring acts). So Maxie Fantano, signature acquired before a gruelling session with moon of anyone's delight that never tires, the world's most deadly female, Roda Randolf, herself a talentless sex-machine built by poet-dreamers like Corst out of a hash-slinging scrubber and layabout, picked up by one, mauled, contracted and passed over to another, publicised flatteringly as malicious, murderous, man-eating, but actually a sweet stupid girl who can't say no, and now on offer by Corst to the lucky boys with the what-with to make cheapies and the know-how to let Corst produce for them. Life was beginning for Corst at forty. His watchword — work before pleasure. He drank a half-tumbler of whisky, toughie Corst, and went out to shout at the world.

It did Corst's slightly enlarged heart good to be in the middle of it all, the buzzing purposeful activity, the great soon-to-be-minting-money studios. If he could get his own script-less (there's a hundred hackeroos for peanuts can script it) film made and meanwhile sublet his valuable studio space for money plus a piece of the incoming pictures, bingo, Hundred Per Cent American was in the business but big. And with Roda tied down with those photographs of her across practically everybody, not to mention the good-wills of the everybodys involved, and the strictly for-nothing price they give him the studios for. Hurray for me, thought Corst, then smiled crookedly, the

[85]

tough butcher's face softening when he thought how, in his he-mannish way, he was fond of that sweet kid Roda (without question the all-time lay of the age).

"Mr. Fantano and Mr. Spirting will be down at eleven, Mr. Corst," said his reserve secretary, the regular horse-face being bedded down after her long night gallop. This one looked more like a cross-eyed dog, big cross spaniel-eyes and daft soft black greased hair hanging sausage-like over her round pink-powdered inflated cheeks. He grunted and passed out into the Sunday morning. Then just so no one should think he was slipping, he banged on the window and when the girl looked up terrified, bawled, "Get me some corfee, some corfee, d'ye hear?"

All this overtime was costing money, so they might as well know that loud-mouthed Corst was in the saddle, their benefactor, the backers' friend, with his cameras coming in tomorrow, shooting Tuesday, a three-week, fifteen-shooting-day schedule, Hundred Per Cent American proudly presenting Roda Randolf in X, an as-yet-unwritten epic of salacious magnificence, using the touched-up old sets which, as Mr. Corst strode across to inspect, included a blue-distempered Nissen hut housing at present a bacon-rind-chewing Old Cock and a tea-brewing Arp.

Everything was crazy in this business, thought Corst, the acid in his stomach starting to trickle backwards to his mouth, but some of the best movies was made on a shoe-string in extenuating circumstances just like his at present, so different (ah memories, memories, the Broad White magical way) from his own famed burlesque shows of the past. Some might say what does it cost to undress the seventy most beautiful dolls in the Union. But plenty of dough can go (and did) on sequin-smothered G-strings and the gaudy magnificence of the New Orleans bordello background or the gipsy encampment.

Gipsies was always a knock-out. Maybe we put Roda in the gipsy encampment, location shot, out there back of the rubbish-tip by those trees, where our story starts, a poor but lovely gipsy maid, dark eyes smouldering, black hair a tangled forest of ensnared something-or-other, her bare feet tap-tapping to the strains of a (post-synchronised) gipsy song wild and stirring, and her would-be lover catching her up into a tempestuous whirling adagio-with-balls-on dance, all done with one guitar-banging flamenco singer from

[87   ]

the Toros Café in Soho. She throws herself down on a bale of hay in a barn (close-shot of panting breasts), flashing eyes moist with mysterious malarkey, lips wet and apart signifying she is passionate against her wilful inclination, a wild untameable woodland creature, pursued by (tap-tap-tap-tap, creaking door, and here he is) the passion-mad gipsy lover determined to get his oats at all costs. Cut back to her breasts panting, eyes flashing, mouth opening, tongue protruding a little, all more than ever (does she or does she not want his cruel caresses?) as he approaches randy and sinister as a big black sleaky rat.

"Dolores," he whispers, "Dolores," a look of pain crossing his face (establishing he wants her so badly) before he flings himself upon her, crazed animal that he is, and they struggle there locked together in a power bigger than both of them, and suddenly her eyes go moist with desire and stop flashing for a moment, she ceases her useless struggle against this thing which is bigger than both of them, and falls back in the hay, her breasts panting still more, while he, knowing he has her at his mercy, burrows his face into her neck, his hungry mouth searching for (but taking a long time to find) hers. A look of pain

[88   ]

crosses her face, torn between duty and desire, but it is nothing compared to the look of pain crossing his face as he is stabbed in the small of the back with a rival's stiletto. The blood runs under the hay as Fernando takes over from the dying Miguel and Roda Randolf is gathered up in his strong arms, cowed and defenceless, her breasts panting like mad, showing as much cleavage as will not embarrass morality above her carefully disarranged blouse.

Given Roda Randolf what did it cost? Peanuts for the extra gipsies, hire a couple of caravans, knock up a barn door and corner out of flats, and how much was hay? Dissolve to something terrific which Maxie and this hack Spirting will knock out between the pair of them, now that he made them a present of the basic situation. *Desire* they would call it. We go into the past seeing that she has always brought out the worst in man, the brute, crazed by her well-stacked charms, etcetera, etcetera, though in the end she must (censor) go into a convent and die repenting.

Corst got some of his greatest ideas just walking around, thinking, thinking. Now a look at the old gear freshened up his thinking, the situations growing out of the existing sets, why get fancy?

Show her in Victorian costume looking virginal, about to be married in Westminster Abbey to some pansy duke, and this strong tough heman Yankee adventurer carries her off under their very eyes. Show her in Ancient Rome, gladiators slaughtering one another viciously for her favours, and the Emperor leering down her dress (those white Roman night-shirts aren't expensive). Put her into the Wild West Badlands and Billy the Kid and Wild Bill shoot it out to make love to Calamity Jane Randolf in the passionate dust of the untamed Mesa. A cinch if you had imagination and weren't afraid to use it.

Look at the minaret or mosque-dome or whatever the hell it was over there. Great idea — put Roda in a harem.

Look at that Army hut. Roda in the Army. Off the cuff — she is walking past the General's headquarters with her cute little fanny beckoning in a friendly fashion, and straightaway he knows she is the girl to stop the leakage of info from the secret school for sabotage he is running here. The General comes out of the Nissen hut. "One second, Sergeant Ogilvie," he says, a sign of what a corker in his eyes.

"You will be dropped at 0020 hours in enemy territory," he says.

"Sir," she says and salutes cutely again but with a steely tightening of her edible mouth.

The General watches her cute little can twitch her back across the parade ground, his wise old face full of admiration.

"What a corker," he sighs, and turns back to the Nissen.

Out of which now comes, Corst observes, a bent big old tramp with a bushy moustache, jetting a gob with remarkable force at least two yards. Followed by a dopy-looking little fellow in a military blouse, smiling all over his moronic face, and drinking from a white enamel mug.

"We'll have a quiet turn round, Arp," the Old Cock says as they enter disturbingly into Corst's glorious exoticolor eye-line. "Hold your horses, Arp, and be ready to come to attention on the command, it's our new lord and master, Mr. Corsir," he shouted the name, coming smartly to attention, and bringing his arm up in a flashy salute. " 'Shun, Arp," he muttered out of the corner of his bacon-greasy mouth, "come to attention, you pull-through rag. At your service, Mr. Corsir. Just on our way to make sure everything is ship-shape and in tip-top order. New broom sweeps clean, Mr. Corsir, and we all got to pull our socks up or maybe heads will fall redundant-like. Look alive there, Arpie. Put nice neat torn-up piles of newspaper in all the toilets for a start. Then report back to me for orders. Scarper now, you silly bleeder, get on, Arp, blast you," he muttered. "Can't you see I want you safe out of the road?"

But Arp was looking at Mr. Corst's socks. Red and yellow check they were, and plainly visible because the well-cut Corst trousers were a bit tucked up that eminent industrialist's behind.

"What are you staring at, you god-damn moron?" bawled Mr. Corst.

"Well put, Mr. Corsir," applauded the Old Cock. "Very well putsir. Now piss off, Arp, before I give you the back of me hand."

He held his dirty fist up under Arp's nose. Not that he needed have done because Arp was going, only socks like that you didn't see every day of the week so why not have a good gander at them while the going was good?

"Nip away smartly, Arp," the Old Cock whispered. "I'll deal with the demon-king meself."

But Arp had suddenly seen what a terrifying red-faced Corst it was, and was pleased to nip off without looking back.

"What you doing in that hut?" asked Corst. "It's company property, ain't it?"

"Oh, every time, Mr. Corsir," assured the Old Cock. "Abso-bloody-lutely company property, from the cracked old windows to the lovely duck-board floor, every nook, chink, and flea-sheltering cranny. But we watchers of the night, Mr. Corsir, me and my young son, Arp, there, poor dumb mental-deefish that he is, we got to kip down somewhere, thus the Nissen hut, thus saving the council our respected employer the capital outlay of proper nancy lodgings with proper beds and chamber pots for us to pass our nights in, which we faithfully spend walking around seeing no one whips the property of our aforesaid respected masters. Of which, if I may be allowed to say so, Mr. Corsir, we are very highly delighted to find you one. And we want you to rest assured, Mr. Corsir, that whatever we done formerly for the council we will now do exactly the same, even more so, for you, for the same money, Mr. Corsir, nobody can say we're on the make, and you can rest with a peaceful head knowing all your great work is not being buggered up by trespassers in the night, thanks to our trained watchman eyes being on the key veef for intruders."

The Old Cock watched Corst's winey face while he babbled (cunning diplomat) to put him against Bates' redundancy notion. But Corst was thinking, quick as lightning, put the two character faces into the story and save a few bucks, who the hell will know, they can be two venerated wise old gipsy kings.

"Tell you what I'll do, Mr. Corsir," said the Old Cock. "I'll tell Mr. Bates you need us and we got to put in more time on the studio guarding, that's what I'm prepared to do for you, sir. Alright, sir?"

But Corst was already past, his soaring imagination in the clouds, his busy red-rimmed eyes glaring round for opportunities, and his trousers still tucked up his kind-hearted old bottom.

Number one, thought the Old Cock, gone off according to plan. Now to face Mr. Clever Bates with the fate accomplee and watch his face drop a few feet. Handling the boss-class came natural to an old soldier. He ambled off whistling, some talk of Alexander, left, right, and some of Hercules, left, right, left, left, of Hector and Lysander and such great names as these, right, left, right. He executed a rather neat change step, then a right wheel, eyes left, onward, ever onward, with a tow-ro-row-ro-row-ro, the British Gren-a-deers.

7

ARP was doing a little quiet rubbish-picking, while the Old Cock searched high and low for the object of his glad news, at this moment taking tea with a certain Mrs. Goffin, a widow lady not less than forty-five and not more than fifty-four who always had been prone for military gentlemen, Goffin himself being a drill sergeant in the Blues (actually a lance-jack in the Artillery, the rest being her girlish swank).

"Thank you for a delightful chat and cup of tea, Mrs. Goffin," said Mr. Bates, wiping a few droplets off his soldierly upper lip. "The canteen will be, I can see already, a well-disciplined lay-out."

"I do a lovely steak and kidney pud," she simpered, "with mashed swedes."

"I can just taste it. Yum, yum" he slapped his

lips, rolling his white-oil eyes sheepily, putting himself out to be friendly on the off-chance something was going for nothing, he having on the qt quite a lecherous tooth for both grub and other, though you would never have dubbed him human by his cold-hearted carry-on at the working man, namely the Old Cock, now on his way to cross swords with the gay Lothario himself, Bates the would-be Goffin-sweeper.

Arp was merrily picking away in the sunshine, a busy cock-sparrow without a care in the world so long as the bits and pieces came up and the clean sack finished up nicely full. As he picked he thought how very often you were quids in not being able to get yourself further in trouble than you already were by careless talk. So long as you carried a stub of pencil there was always a handy scrap of paper for you to write down ten cigs or six rashers should someone not know what you wanted by pointing and smiling, or should the unforgivable happen and you forget and start out to ask and finish up gibbering like a chimp.

And think of the trouble you kept out of. When you kept quiet you became like the furniture or a corpse, they thought you couldn't think or hear either, copping a terrific surprise when you noticed such things as special red and yellow check socks which meant something special you weren't supposed to know about. But you knew all right — they came as a Christmas present although Arp would never have wore them because they were a bit too flashy for work, all and sundry would have taken the mike out of him when they saw the great red and yellow squares, very sporting times. But a lovely present. For who? Mr. Corst, that's who. From who? Mr. Corst was a man with plenty of friends to go in for flash presents of that kind. Arp jabbed viciously at a pineapple tin so that his picker went straight into it.

With his experience Arp could comb a dump in no time at all, a new record-holder in the rubbish-picking. It was his special method that did it, up and down, up and down, don't be tempted to dive about here and there but carefully up and down, ploughing the dump for its pickable bits, none of your hit and miss ways. And it was tidier and quicker in the end. And you felt you'd made a job of it. That was the important thing. You had your self-respect, regardless of checked socks, grey coats, three-piece suites in real hide-type rexine finish, grained and smelling expensive, like that one in the shop where the man came forward to push him away from the window. Only the shape of the back should have been different. The settee is better with a higher back. How do you *know* all these funny things, Arp?

Mind your own business.

Pick, pick, jab, jab, got you, you old marrow bone with the marrow all gone. Get in the bag. Arp isn't a man to be trifled with while sorting out the whys and wherefores of a rubbish dump.

The Old Cock saw Bates loping off in the direction of the front gates now being oiled and painted up ready for action. He was prepared to track him down and have the redundancy business out there and then, when his ever-hungry nostrils were assailed by the mouth-watering perfume of steak and onions cooking gently not too far away. Always on the recky for the grub stakes, his tape-worm stomach gurgling and his mouth full of savoury saliva, the Old Cock stood stock-still snuffling at the air like a police-dog. The ghost of former busy canteen cooks stalked the place. Smoke rose from the long-empty kitchens. Peering through the dusty window he saw no ghost but the shapely bulk of Mrs. Goffin bending over the oven with a shelf pulled out, tiddling up a great dish of tinned steak and onion. Quick as a flash he spied the empty red-labelled tins, the sliced kidneys on the table, and the rolled-out dough waiting to encase the delectable combination for boiling. Pulling his choker tight and pushing his cap back off his forehead he turned into the kitchen, an old soldier, strictly on the make and as cocky as they come.

As soon as Mrs. Goffin turned round, her proud bosom drawn up matron-style and her still rich brown hair piled into a spilling pyramid above her duster-turban, and faced him four-square across the kitchen, the Old Cock knew it called for a lady-like approach.

"Morning, mam," he said, touching his peak and bending his head to show respect for her toney frontage. "Any complaints? Fire drawing well, stove-pipe unblocked, dust removed? I'll clear these off for a start," he continued, collecting up the big tins and thinking nice little windfall for Arp.

"Any problems, mam," he said, leering politely at her, "just call for the studio guard, known as

Cocky to me friends among which I will be proud to count yourself."

"Mrs. Goffin," said Mrs. Goffin, thinking he carries himself well for an old 'un and there's no smoke without a bit of spark somewhere.

"Mrs. Goffin," he repeated, looking her boldly in the face, red-cheeked from bending over a hot stove day after day. "Mr. Goffin is a lucky man," he said, running his eyes down her oak-bedstead shape.

"Sergeant Goffin," she corrected, "late of the Blues. He passed over seven year back."

"I'm sorry to hear it, mam," said the Old Cock looking down to the floor, suddenly saddened. "Making a steak pud?" he inquired, his eyes on the table.

"Steak and kid, with mashed swedes," she said, "one of my specials."

"Me favourite," he said, "me dear old lady, bless her departed soul, always give it to me of a Thursday. Duty calls, mam," he sighed, "I'll be off."

"Pop in later," she said, "I'll save you a spot."

"A heart as big as a horse," he said, gave her a straight look and kissed his cunning hand.

What-ho for the merry widow, thought the

Old Cock, glancing through the window as he passed, catching her naughty old eye which looked away when he tipped her a wink. Give me the ripe ones any time, he thought, they're grateful and they can cook. We'll look into that later after we've wrapped ourself round her gorgeous pud. Look out, Bates, the Camels are coming, you slimy skin-and-gristle tripe-hound, here comes Mr. Corsir's bodyguard and the darling of the goffin-girls, the cocky Old Cock with the winning ways and the giant portion of kate and sidney in the offing. Let me get at the jumped-up toffy-nose.

It took him half an hour before Bates was in a nice position for the assault to be launched. A couple of times, true, the Old Cock could have walked straight up to him, whipped him round by the sharp shoulder-blades, and pitched straight into him, but why throw away your advantage? Which was now, with Bates chatting away to Mr. Corsir, the pair of them blown up like a couple of giant balloons.

"All the timber stripped down and taken to the big shed," puffed Corst through his cigar. "All reclaimed timber saves us dough."

"Without doubt, Mr. Corst," said Bates, lighting up at his master's brilliance. "The council wants you to have the free use of any amenities the property offers."

"The trouble I'm getting them out of taking over the lousy joint, I should hope so," grumbled Corst smokily. "They been losing a fortune here in local taxes. Next thing you know my good friends the council will be putting up the taxes."

"You will have your little joke, Mr. Corst," giggled Bates, the toadying snurge. "*There* you are," he hissed suddenly, seeing the Old Cock.

"Reporting for duty, Mr. Corsir," said the Old Cock with stiff respect, pointedly ignoring Bates. "The ropy bits of timber will be forthwith gathered into the big shed, under the personal supervision of your own appointed watchman and guard, namely myself."

He looked at Bates, daring him to argue the point.

"Now that's anticipation," said Corst admiringly. "Guess the old guy does a good job considering his age," he said, ready to rush onward. "We get him with the rest of the joint, right? Saves us a few bucks, and he knows his way around. Right, Bates?"

And he carried on with his round of good

works, Lord Bountiful Corst, the Peg of the Old Cock's heart.

"Right, Bates?" said the Old Cock. "Put that up your redundant flue and smoke it."

"Watch your lip, you old rotter," hissed Bates, and you could tell he was feeling very curses-foiled-again. "I'll have you yet, you drunken old loafer."

"Look, Bates," said the Old Cock, "I don't want no trouble with you because it only inter-feres with me important duties to the council's new tenant, my friend and patron, Mr. Corsir. But if you don't stop sorting me out, Bates, old chap, I'm going to take that badge of yours on its peaked inspectorial cap, and stuff it clean up your jacksie. So give over annoying me, do, there's a good fellow, you lousy, rotten, stinking, stuck-up, bullying bleeder you. You're full of piss and wind, Batesy, old champ. Go and get cleared out."

With a dignified look the Old Cock turned smartly round and marched off, already won-dering if he hadn't gone a little overboard in his description, altogether too far in his righteous wrath against a man who was, after all, highly superior to one who remained the lowest grade temporary non-pensionable civil servant ever devised by this or any other council. Long live Mr. Corsir, prayed the Old Cock fervent with fear, gord spare Mr. Corsir, the Old Cock's personal defence-of-the-realm act. And he decided to spend the rest of the morning hard-working the timber off the flats in the big shed. Further than working no working man can go to keep his job, he thought, wiping the sweat off his swollen nose with the back of his hand and listening to his stomach grumbling sadly in the distance.

Half an hour later, roll on dinner-time, the Old Cock thought as he heaved the four-by-two back supports off the rotting canvas flats. Willing is one thing, but this is getting beyond all reason, they don't want to start expecting this kind of service every day of the week. Still, worth it to get in with friends at Corse (that's what they call a pun) and thus get settled into another cushy few years. No good being too proud when you don't have the muscles to back it up with.

Roll on dinner-time and we'll have a quiet natter with Ma Goffin, a few years back it would have been La Goffin alright, she's put a bit of weight on but that won't hurt. He stood up

[105]

groaning as his back creaked straight. As he wiped his forehead a wood-pigeon up in the old shed roof started to coo. "That wouldn't be a bad idea," he said aloud. "Me and Arp knock up a cage for a few pigeons, racing for preference, more money in them, like them pedigree pigeons we ate up that time we had that house near Loos for a billet, they was worth a lot or so their Froggy dad said when he come back for the bones. That's all there was because we'd eaten the bloody lot. Cried like a woman he did."

The pigeon fluttered down to peck in the mould the disturbed flats had pushed up, its mate following closely. "Bet he's the old man," the Old Cock said. "Look at his wicked beady eye. Look at the way he's chasing her. After her, mate. Leave her alone you, dirty redundant old sod. Who was that fellow used to race pigeons all the way from Rheims? There's money in them al-right. You can be independent with a good bunch of pigeons. Leave her alone you randy old joker. It must be treading time for pigeons. Unlike us, they only fancy it at a certain time. Roll on dinner-time."

8

Don't think Bates didn't know his business, because he did. He hadn't been lick-spittling and bottom-polishing for years for nothing, not him. He was a first-class, number one, grade A diabolical monster, and once he got his knife into the Old Cock he wasn't going to take it out until the poor victim was lumbered good and proper. Being, into the bargain, a book-of-rules master's man and needled to death by the Old Cock's impudence, Bates, a proper prodnose for correct procedure, had (always in accordance with regulations) gone out of his way to put in report after lying report to the effect that the Old Cock is definitely lagging behind on routine, is slap-dash in his carry-on, immoral and not to put too fine a point on it, a ripe old candidate for the dreaded redundancy stakes.

So there is Bates, insinuating and button-holing, poisoning ear after ear in the sanitary department with his endless narking and dark warnings as to typhoid being forthcoming from neglect of rubbish tips, all due to drunk-in-charge minor officials of the council not carrying out their duties within the meaning of the phrase, not to mention rats, mice, and other vermin, with over and above them the dark spectre of the evil Old Cock looming like King Plague upon a dump which would otherwise blossom like a rose in sensible tidiness, being a credit to the entire department, thus the elected council, thus the body politic of the people only with whom is progress.

Never mentioning, of course (wily artful underhanded Bates) that his own bestial dustmen were entirely to blame with their careless methods of disposal of the ordures in their charge and therefore under the command of Bates himself. Never a word about the dissolute dustmen with their cavalier carrying-on, their vile un-Britishness being the principal source of any complaint which might be lodged at the general conduct of the corporation rubbish dump which, try as he may, the Old Cock, even with the expert assistance of a class tradesman like Arp, was a mere Canute against the waves which were bashing the place into very chaos under Bates' very white witch-hunting nose.

For weeks now the Bates needle was working overtime with his tireless refrain that the dump should be closed down and covered up, and this message had in fact reached the higher levels of assistants in the surveyor's department as well as the more appropriate sewage and sanitary officers their revered selves, even to the extreme of a sarky inter-departmental memo, Evans Sanitary to Mitchell Survey, what alternative to Tip 4 is suggested? And back came the reply, a custard pie slap in the Welsh face of Evans Sanitary, viz., with land values and building land shortage be-ing what they are, no suggestions for alternative tip location as yet, so put that in your reeky pipe and choke on it, you Welsh would-be depart-mental hurdle-jumper. In the teeth of which higher political friction Bates could only look the small fry he was, and the rubbish dump remain its old self, a sacrifice on the altar of the foul Old Cock.

No wonder then that the Old Cock stuck in the Bates gullet, like an old toe-rag baked in a pie, for Bates was till now strictly *persona grata* round the council offices, both for his years of faithful unstinting service and for his knowledge of local sewage farming which was second to none, for had he not worked his way up from a mere sewage farm-worker to higher things? His permanent local government service rating was an achievement commanding a certain respect you would think. But not from the loopy Old Cock, the foul-mouthed commoner who respected neither man nor permanent official, but merely cringed before the frown of authority, fiddled his way round the rules, won what he could from the council's perquisites, flogged whatever came to hand, introduced vagrants of a dumb nature to the amenities of his official place, and manoeuvred himself like the dirty rivulets of water running out of the dump on a wet day into a nice comfy ditch where he could pig it at his pleasure with no one to say him nay other than duty-worshipping Bates, the council's king-pin.

Why, wondered Bates, philosophical for a passing moment in the hurly-burly of his working day, why did some live life as a service to something higher while others scattered its oportunities to the four winds like a bundle of discarded duplicate forms which must remain forever un-fulfilled-in with promise?

Why (to bring it down to earth) should the Old Cock have a bloody good bloody easy bloody high old time of it while he knocked himself out worrying over his responsibilities for yet a few more years in this vale of care at the end of which is a nice little semi-detached house, paid for and inhabited by retired Bates, waiting for a respectable funeral purveyor to cart him off to the council cemetery, rest in peace, thou true and faithful public servant.

What kind of life was it, all said and done, what kind of life could you call it (without prejudice now), what style of a life had a Bates lived to make him tolerant and kind and content? What was there in its over-all arithmetic calculated to prove that back-sliders should not cop back-handers from the time-serving officers of authority?

First the four-room house, bath in the kitchen to a rattle of tin on stone floor, mother's cooking fried bread, dad's a casual signing on day after day for work as and when, sister Susan an usherette night after night in a smoky dreamland and going to the pictures on her night off,

elder sister Irene fought hard for her virtue
(within the basic meaning of the act) till tired
out with waiting for Mr. Right she capitulated
to Mister Wrong (as it turned out) a garage
mechanic who copped two years in the end for
complicity in car-pinching (he sprayed, changed
the licence plates and filed off the engine number
for no more money than it cost to get stinko
twice a week), and he himself, Tiny Bates, the
baby of the family, a council man ever since he
clocked in, a snot-nosed shivering five at the
council school, class of Miss L. Winter, a hard
cane-user who hated the grubby little suet-pud-
smelling male piglets snuffling *ar farver witch
arty heffin* morning after grey school-room morning.

Such the earlier life and bleak times of Bates,
today an admitted success with a secure place in
the bowling club, recognised down at the Con-
servative-Unionist billiard-room and bar, well
ahead in the snooker championship, slightly
sharpish some might say but by and large a decent hail-fellow-well-met so why not invite him
to put up for the brotherhood, why not speak
to that snob town clerk Gillespie.

Little did they know what happened to Irene's

hubby, and how Su finished up although she was always the quiet one of the family, and what he did that time they all went down to Southend for the day with that other kid (but no one ever found out). Certainly no one could say that his missus wasn't presentable even if she did have her inside out after that first one went wrong since when she sometimes got these ice-cold white-hot rages, without a word would put his tea on the table and fly upstairs. But an Englishman's home is his castle so enough of that, it was none of their business, and if Gillespie didn't want him in the lodge he would definitely put up for the Liberal Club. Let the snooker team lose its best man. Gillespie might be a big noise on the council but in billiards he was a mere office boy, which brings you back to the unfairness of it all, crawling to a nobody in a high place while a nobody with no standing at all (meaning the Old Cock) gives you the rough side of his tongue through a slob-bery unbuttoned lip. Gillespie was his crown of thorns, but the Old Cock was the insult over and above the injury.

Now Bates, reviewing the situation, had to ad-mit that the Old Cock was more clever (cun-ning was the better word) than you would credit, the way he had wormed through the good books of no less than Mr. Corst the producer by endless ruses for ingratiating himself with the bighearted, deep-pocketed, cigar-hoisting American foreigner, good at his own job doubtless, but no match for the guile of an old British soldier with one foot in the grave and the other firmly planted in the door of the canteen kitchen (encouraged, believe it or not, by Mrs. Goffin, in all other ways an efficient and admirable servant of the council, alas, entirely taken in by the fulsome flattery and thieving compliments of an unscrupulous oniony devil making sheep's eyes while he wolfs her delightful spotted dog or treacly tart).

Which brings us (with a livid revengeful Bates never far away) to the well-known bandit and his silent though deadly adjutant stuffing theirselves to the gills with the proceeds of the Old Cock's as yet platonic friendship with La Goffin. The rafters of their hide-out Nissen ringing with good cheer as the Old Cock slaps his thighs and laughs in a coarse asthmatical way.

"Never saw such goings-on since old Macdockery died," the Old Cock wheezed. "The coming and going, the to-ing and fro-ing, the shagging and shouting, the eating and drinking. I thought our number was up when that Corse lot come here, but frankly, Arpie, I never had such a high old time since Armistice night when we got the freedom of the village and they give us the brothel to ourself, no one out of uniform admitted. The ving blong run free like water in the trenches. La Goffin is something special in judies, Arp, she is a remarkable woman, none of your soppy bits of fluff. Eat up your pork pie, Arpie. You like pork pie, don't you, Arpie, all thanks to La Goffin. Tuck in, cockie. There's plenty more where that come from. Long live the film business, Arpie. Let's drink to that."

The Old Cock stood up over the groaning board on which several barely touched portions of pork and veal-and-ham pie yet remained, a generous heel of cheddar, a half-cut loaf, a saucer of collected assorted pats of butter and marge depending on whether they'd been salvaged from the workers' canteen or the executives' restaurant, and believe it or not, three barely gnawed drumsticks and a large piece of slightly-off boiled salmon.

Arp stopped chewing on a mouthful of pork pie, peppery, jellyish and succulent, picked up his cup (one of two borrowed from La Goffin by

[115]

nature's gentleman the Old Cock) and held it up high.

"Only a mere few days," the Old Cock chortled, "and already we have learned to love them. Let us pray the Lord spare them to us for many a long cushy month, you to make your fortune on the refuse they throw up so extravagant, and me to make the grade with La Goffin and provide meself with a ripe old age. It's years since I enjoyed a bit of Scotch salmon so much as this, Arp," he said, spitting a few little bits here and there round the table. "Try a drumstick, Arp, and give me just a thimbleful more hot tea to freshen up me cup. We come a long way together, old fellow, from cabbage and bacon. Dig in the scrape, Arp, take plenty. A heart of solid twenty-two carat butter she has, she's an institution, that woman, the things common louts say in front of her, Arp, I blush for the mannerless hounds, straight I do. I sorted out one of the pigs yesterday, but she says not to worry, she's used to their talk, it runs off like water on a duck's back. I don't mind telling you she's got one of the biggest backsides I ever give a slap to. Sporting old puss, she is, Arpie, 'Paws off, Pompie,' she says, but I see she liked it. She's coming down to the boozer with me one of these nights and don't look at me so old-fashioned, Arp, old sport, I know the proper carry-on with a jane of her class. Two stouts and off for a spot of slap and tickle all being well. What do *you* want, mate? This here is private property, reserved for the brigade of night guards."

A pimply young fellow in a yachting blazer with two silver buttons missing, a yellow silk scarf (with a tea-stain) tied loosely round his unappetising neck, preened himself in the door.

"Get down to the wardrobe straightaway," he ordered, "there's a lot of junk wants clearing out," talking as if there was a bad smell under his nose, and there wasn't to speak of.

"Bless your honour," hee-hawed the Old Cock in old Irish, "and what does your honour do wasting his great talents on the likes of us? Get out of it, you little git," he shouted, lapsing into normal, "before I kick your green teeth down your gullet. Uppity tea-boys make me puke. Get in some service, spotty, before you go ordering about. Come on, Arp, duty calls."

"It's not a mahogany job with mirror doors, you know, Arp," he said pensively as they walked along. "It's where they keep a fortune in old clothes, all colours of the rainbow. I was only thinking yesterday when I took a screw round the place, old Rambam would pay a few bob for them bits and pieces. Maybe they're going to get rid of the old rags, Arp. It could put us right in the business. Maybe we got it more cushy than we even thought. Be nice if Mr. Corsir out of the kindness of his heart done us up a bit nice-looking in a couple of commissionaire's uniforms to put on a bit of sprawnce for the visiting dignities. How do you fancy yourself, Arpie, in one of them gold braid jobs with more gongs on your chest than the Duke of Wellington?"

When they got there and before they could ask what the job was the missus of the place, a thin girl with one of them rat-trap mouths you wouldn't want to get your finger caught in, pointed to a pile of night-shirts and grubby turbans being handed out to all and sundry.

"Drop it," she said when the Old Cock pinched where her bottom ought to be, more out of kindness to her than out of interest on his part. "I know all about dirty old men like you. Get into those costumes and quick about it."

"Going to tuck us into bed, lady," insinuated the Old Cock, seeing at once that she was on the strait-laced side. "The nice lady is going to pop us straight into a warm beddy-byes, Arpie, old china," he leered. "Take your knickers off, Arpie, and we'll see what we can do for madam."

"Put them on over your normal garments," she said acidly. "You've got nothing to show I want to look at."

She got them out of there, pushing the Old Cock's thieving hands off a genuine ostrich-feather boa, in five minutes flat.

"Here we are out of work again but who cares?" said the Old Cock. "Look, Arp, in an old Persian Market. Da dadada da dadada," he sang, belly-dancing. "Just like a couple of Messpot woggies out on a spree. Here." He hoiked up the skirts of his costume. "Knees up, Mother Brown, for the love of Allah, your drawers are hanging down, for the love of Allah. Let's have a bit of a knees-up, Arp. Put your turban straight, soppy, and let's get a move on out of it. I see young snot-nose on our trail again. Who wants to work? You can drive a horse to water but you can't make him take a bath."

When they stopped running the Old Cock leaned wheezing against a corrugated wall and looked Arp over. "You don't half look daft in that get-up, Arp," he breathed. "Ay-ay — what's that pretty little house on wheels over there? Better look into this."

He tip-toed over, his sure nose for irregular goings-on pointing like a retriever's till he was close enough to snoop through the window of the doll's house with its proudly silver-starred door inscribed *Roda Randolf.*

"Scarper, Arp," he said, recoiling sharply, "you're too young. Get fell in back at the hut," and Arp bolted like a hare thinking Bates.

But no. Within an unidentified electrician whose name (if we knew it) should be inscribed with other distinguished octopuses was gathering several handfuls of the famous film-star's famous figure while she relaxed, breathing hard and wondering why doesn't he hurry, I wish I could say no but since I can't please hurry, don't waste valuable time whispering sweet nothings into my shell-like ears.

"Reaching for his flies now," muttered the Old Cock. "What-ho," he applauded, "I'm proud of you, old sport — I know when I'm not wanted. I'll just go and have a word with La Goffin," he thought, a bit stalky. What a bottom, none of your little peaches. A ripe old melon.

Those of us who have suffered from the mystic drag a woman can exercise over the hackles of a man's mind and so on, will tremble now knowing that the Old Cock is being, as they say, inexorably drawn by destiny upon the delectable rocks (meaning La Goffin) of which the recently-witnessed goings-on had, as they say, inexorably reminded him. So much for him as he slinks, an aged but eager tom, mangy, scarred and rattling like a couple of ball-bearings in an aluminum cup, en route to the sugared cat-nip mountains of Cloud Goffin-land.

Meanwhile Arp didn't go back at once but swanked around in the costume which, even if the Old Cock thought soppy, at least made you feel like somebody else. If only they had an old false beard to spare and a red wig he could pass anyone and, no matter how well they knew him, if asked, they would never in their life guess it was Arp.

Passing Mr. Corst's busy office he saw the devoted producer himself shouting into a telephone, the spit spraying, his forehead sweating, eyes bulging like sugar plums.

"But, Harry," came the voice, still strong through the closed windows, "you have my personal word the movie will be finished on time."

Everybody, thought Arp, has got somebody to shout at except me. As he walked back, the skirts of his costume flickering in the breeze, he shouted in his mind at several people. They just laughed back, pleased to hear from him after so long. He did not see in the vicinity of the canteen the threatening figure of the doomed Old Cock wending his randy way to a buttocky Waterloo. But Bates did.

9

IT'S UP TO YOU, ladies and gents of the jury, to judge in all fairness whether what follows is in itself culpable, or whether rather the fact that it leads up to the Old Cock getting the push is just another example of the stinking hypocrisy of the official mind which, while getting up to I wouldn't like to say what under their whited sheets in their safe suburban nights, puts on a celluloid collar in the morning and with a tight greasy mind goes prodnosing around with a black note-book and a stub of pencil picking up evidence of immorality and inefficiency on the part of war veterans and other true men of the world.

Here is your Bates pussy-footing his treacherous way after the gay Old Cock, pursuing a vindictive plan to produce in triplicate a detailed account of how that hero spends his so-called working day so that if any dare say after that there is no call for redundancy then his name is not Bates. There he slinks, the vile copper's nark, behind a concealing wall to watch and wait for his unsuspecting quarry, now merrily lolloping forward, ladies and gents, to pass the time of day with a fellow-worker who happens to be a female of the species and in consequence slightly deadly.

Round the kitchen door peered the bleary ripe face of the costumed Old Cock, able for anything and twice as ready as a young 'un.

"Who dragged you in?" inquired La Goffin sternly twinkling as the Old Cock sidled back into her life. "What dirty old ditch did you crawl out of like a maggot in a turnip all dressed up and nowhere to go, you old Sheik of Araby? You don't half look a scream, sergeant-major." Because the lying Old Cock had spun her a fine yarn about his days of glory and if her late old man was a sergeant he had to go one better.

"Into your tent I'll creep," sang the Old Cock, fixing her with an oily eye and a tasty smile. "One night when you're asleep."

"Nark it, sergeant-major," she said, turning away and bending over a sack of spuds so that her dress hoiked up a good half-foot and her plump white back thigh hit him plum in the peepers. "I don't appreciate that sort of a joke," she said, bending over a little further.

"If I catch you bending, I'll saw your leg right off," sang the Old Cock liltingly as he crept on silent pigeon-toes up to her beckoning backside. "Knees up, knees up," whistled the Old Cock grimly through his teeth as he prepared for mortal combat.

"Not that a person could take much harm from an old tomcat like you," continued Mrs. Goffin, reaching right deep down into the sack so that he could get an eyeful. "You're all bark and no bite," she said, and then screamed, stood upright, turned and clopped the Old Cock flat across the kisser all in one graceful movement. "You dirty old sod," she said, her face boiled beetroot. "I'm going to report you for that."

"No harm meant, old dear," whined the Old Cock, "none taken, I'm sure, mam. I give way to a sudden impulse. Who wouldn't be brought on by such a view, I ask you, in all fairness?"

"Never mind that," she said quietly, turning away. "You can just drop all that. I ought to report it."

"No need, madam," said a choked official voice

from the door. "The incident did not pass unnoticed."

It was black Bates the well-known killjoy, personal enemy to the Old Cock, his bastard self. "That puts the kybosh on you, you old swine," he spat. "The council won't wear immorality, that they won't countenance."

"Ow, me tape-worm," screamed the Old Cock, and collapsed on the floor groaning.

Through his squinting eyes he spied La Goffin coming sympathetically down towards him. Slightly opening his right eye he saw Bates happy and vengeful turn and stomp out of the door. As the door swung back with a crash he sat up creaking, dimly and sadly gazing into La Goffin's face.

"Poor old fellow," she cooed, great bleeding heart of soft female sympathy that she was. "Are you in pain, dearie?" she asked.

"Horrible pain," whimpered the Old Cock, pressing his stomach. "The creature's crying for grub."

"Could you take a little Irish stew?" she inquired tenderly.

"Just a little," grunted the Old Cock, getting up by way of a good grip on her lovely arms.

"I'm finished, me old dear," he sighed, as she

dished up the savoury mess. "Give us a crust of bread," he added, "there's a good girlie. Me job's scuppered, but san fairy ann. Now this is a real old stew this is — with a dumpling, I see. I've had me lot, Madam Goffin, me perishing lot."

"You can call me Emily," Mrs. Goffin said, her eyes modestly fixed upon the off-white baker's tin loaf she was hacking.

"I never meant to get you into trouble," she said.

"Me fatal weakness done me down," he gobbled gallantly through a stuffed mouth. "I blame only me own doggish self for this calamity. A tiny spot more stew would maybe soften the blow, but not I fear prevent it proving fatal."

10

THE QUESTION IS," said the Old Cock, pulling at his bushy moustache, lifting his upper lip and picking his craggy front teeth with a black finger-nail, "have I the right, Arp? Do I, a tyke with me life like a pooch's tail behind me, have the cheek to expect such a thing? Do I, Arp, an elderly geezer no matter which way you look at it, a crusty, dusty, doss-house joe with less to come than I've had already and no more blood or spunk in me than will keep a small house-mouse in fair trim, a rotten old wreck, Arp, with a shocking amount of sinning to his credit I assure you, a tired tinker on the stony road towards an iron cot in the work-house and skilly twice a day, dare I, Arp, a shaky old shagbag of fleas and farts, ask a lady fair and kind, I did but see her passing by, to honour me with her plump spud-scrubbing hand in what I can only in all fairness call holy matrimonial suicide?"

He leaned back on his bunk, the pink bags under his eyes drooping with sadness, his great battered nose stark in the slough of despond which served him for a face.

"When she give me one of them dripping-toast looks, Arp, me courage comes up like a cocks-comb and I reckon nothing venture nothing gain, good-bye caution, over the top we go. Oh, Arp, Arp, Arpie, me old cock-sparrow, what a deal of trouble a joker stores up for hisself when, all forgetful of the argee-bargee to come he shoots his load of woe into the plummy heart of a friendly doll. What a deep drain-hole of desperate hope springs eternal in the human breast when you catch a quick gander of all that lush love patiently awaiting in the pantry of her lily-white paps. What turmoil in the cock-eyed brain-box at the very thought of it. Little do you reckon how she's got you by the short hairs, very soon you will be bathing like a fairy, bashing Brylcreem by the bottleful, sweet stinking as a pansy in a pot. Stop, Arp, stop for a tick and look it over sensible-like, take yourself in hand and wonder why. Give yourself a roasting for your stupid-cupid notions. A woman's not the answer to the loneliness of man. But, Arp, you can't defeat it, the beating, booming, heart-quake, the barmy love-light bursts right through your glims. You had better get a tape-worm, grow it, train it, love it, feed it on your vitals, it's anyway you reckon it less harmful than a jane."

The Old Cock fell back in tragic desperation at the sore straits his passion had sailed him into. He refused both tea and beer from Arp's hands, taking only a crusty heel of french loaf and gnawing on it with his discoloured front teeth like an enormous hoary rat. After a few tense moments he put the crust down and began to sing in a quavering voice which drippingly dragged the words out till, stretched to breaking point, they no longer meant anything less or more than his caterwauling love-sickness.

"I-yi av erda myviss singina ittsa luff songa to da rozah. I-yi-aach."

He sat up ceasing the song as he jettisoned a high-speed gob through the door.

" No good getting down-hearted, Arpie, old son," he said. "It's a nice bright morning and I might as well muster up all the joy de verve I can cotton on to and get stuck into life as she has to be lived — meaning take a crack at La Goffin and see if she's going to give me the pleasure of her company down to the Bunch of Grapes to-night. Being as she's a woman of the world, Arp, she will have forgive me goosing her slightly in the passion of the moment. Who knows, Arp, whether she is not waiting for this very occasion. Lovely night oh night of bliss," he sang. "You can't beat the good old songs when it comes to talking about the old udder in a nice refined kind of way."

After damping the corner of his small grey towel in the still-warm water in the kettle, the Old Cock carefully wiped the corners of his face out.

"A cat's lick and a promise," he said, "the car-case is a shade rank, but the soul is in good work-ing order — though the heart," (he let rip a sin-ister wheeze), "is as black as the ace of spades. I'm a dirty old bugger, Arp," he chortled, and ambled out, his big bent shoulders forwards like a pouncing vulture.

The Old Cock mumbling, "I give it to Dolly because she was jolly," strolled along saluting a passing studio dignitary, a round, red-faced, bald-headed property man named Walt who was (the

Old Cock admitted) in the same class as himself for scrounging.

"No wonder, Arp," he explained, "eighteen year in the Buffs. You can't beat the army training."

Walt stopped dead in his tracks.

"You can help me, I shouldn't wonder, Old Cock," he said, a vague calculating look in his eyes. "I need a sheep."

"Living or dead?" asked the Old Cock.

"All alive-o," replied Walt, "and preferably with a black patch, you know the style, black patch, nothing too special, worth half-a-crack if you can put me on to it."

"Straight across the allotments," replied the Old Cock, "down the little dip leads into the quarry, there's a few sheep round there property of a high-class butcher buys the poor little bleeders on the hoof so his mutton will be prime fresh-killed stuff, the murdering capitalist."

"Much obliged," Walt said, fishing for the half-crown in his waistcoat pocket. "Might as well get rich while we can, this is a proper Fred Karno outfit here, I tell you, won't be long before the balloon goes up."

"No trouble, I trust?" asked the Old Cock,

thinking he's taking his time to find that half-a-crack.

Walt pinched his nose and pulled an unseen chain. "Complete cock-up," he said, "they don't know their backsides from breakfast-time. Films — they couldn't use a box Brownie." He gave the Old Cock the coin at last. "Enjoy it while you can."

Certainly the distant figure of Corst, his great beaked head bent, his horse-faced secretary distressfully at his elbow waiting for the next bark, was no encouragement to optimistic investors. But naturally we have all got our troubles and naturally the bigger we are the bigger they are.

Enough of that, thought the Old Cock, the gay *caballero,* why worry so long as we've got enough to purchase a red rose or two for La Goffin to wear in her pearly teeth and rich ripe hair, if only there was any roses here to be bought.

"Every morn I bring thee violets," the Old Cock sang out loud.

But it was not to be that morning. That morning was one of the most violet-less ever, a morning in which anything smelling so sweet would have had its odoriferous life blown right out of it by the catastrophic entrance of a pug-nosed postman with a sack of birthday cards, letters from loved ones and postal orders for some, but for the hell-bent Old Cock nothing but a tidgy little buff manila envelope, specked with straw and bearing the arms and dignity of the popularly elected council its holy self. The Old Cock, the sense of doom heavy upon him, turned from the path of dalliance and returned to the Nissen. When he got there he still hadn't opened the envelope.

Arp was sorting lemonade bottles in different sizes into appropriate boxes. Under the new order there was a small fortune in bottles to be picked up around the place and he had opened a department (two large apple boxes) specialising in them. He washed them in the pail, wiped them over, scrubbing them well with a worn lavatory brush so that sparkling like rock crystal and labelless, they were a joy to behold.

The Old Cock came in holding the envelope straight out in front of him, shaking it up and down jerkily as if to improve the mixture it contained, or at least change his typed name upon it to someone, anyone, else's.

"Maybe it's a citation, Arp," he said, "or a mention in dispatches, a commendation of gallantry to one entitled to put up the old Mons star upon his noble breast. Maybe it's a free voucher for baccy or baby's orange juice which I tried once down at me daughter's and gives me a belly-ache, or a one-way train ticket to Skegness, or a coupon for the Irish Sweepstake with a seven in it, my lucky number, or a personal invitation to the mayor's parlour for tea and hot crumpet, or a polite request to open a bazaar or a sale of work in aid of the old age pensioners, or it could be anything like that, Arp, only it isn't."

He tossed the envelope wearily on to Arp's knocked-up box table (to which in the passage of time a black-and-white check lino top had been added) and stood staring at it silently for a while.

When Arp made to pick it up he shouted, "Don't touch it, kamerad, it might explode in your face and blow your nose down your gullet. It's not fair for you to take that risk, Arpie, old scout. The bomb has dropped and it's got no-body else's name and number on it but yours truly. Say la gar, Arp, say la sodding gar."

Then he calmly picked up the letter, tore the end of it clean off, drew the folded message out delicately by one corner, opened it with the tips of his fingers as if still on the look-out for booby-traps, adjusted it to the proper distance for his long sighted vision, and recited with cold precision:

"The question of your employment with this authority in the category of night-watchman (sanitary dept.) temporary non-pensionable grade has now been reviewed, and it is my duty to inform you that in view of changing circumstances this appointment has been classified as redundant as from the end of the current month.

"The departmental head has asked me to thank you for your loyal service.

"Yours faithfully,

"I can't read his bastard name," the Old Cock ran on regretfully, "looks like Picklewater. I never met the departmental head hisself. I think I'll frame this, Arp, so I'll have something to read while I'm starving to death. It puts paid to any jigging thoughts of romance I might have. La Goffin, Emily, good-bye."

The Old Cock settled into a dark brown study, his murky eyes looking right through Arp to some not far off workhouse in a setting of dusty ever-green laurel bushes.

"Come and see me some time, Arp," he said some minutes later. "I'll be sucking bread and skimmed milk into me gummy mouth and slobbering like a puking babe, but if I'm not too far gone in the head I'll be glad to see you. May Bates drop dead on the deck in horrible torment, the dirty black traitor, never trust a council man, Arp, or a nancy-boy, their livers are white and their hearts shrunk and black as a mouldy pea. I give that louse of a master's bum-boy as fair a deal as me own flesh and blood, he was a child to me, Arp, leastways his rubbish was, I was a flaming wet-nurse to it. Yet he come like a thief in the night, copped me by the cobblers, knackered me, stoned me and cast me out a poor orphan of the storm. It's sufficient to bring tears to the eyes of a brass monkey."

He wiped the eye from which a large oily drop had obediently started.

"Funny thing, Arp, the left eye was always more prone than the right, even in a gas attack, the old left would be running away while the right didn't even know what was happening. Before the issue gas-mask come through we made water on a hankie (if available) and stuck it over our gobs, Arp. You might say filthy, but the ammonia suck up the foul noxious fumes and anyway your own stink is a bloody sight better than the Kaiser's, poor old imperial chap sodding about in his model market-garden and pegging before the next lot was ready. It's not right, Arp — they should give us old soldiers a bit more consideration."

Who knows how much longer the Old Cock might have shilly-shallied round the shell-hole which the letter-bomb had blasted, scuttling here and there in his personal limbo for enough bits to bridge the gap, had an ardent trade-unionist not arrived, a shop steward, worried for some days now whether those black-legged boys Arp and the Old Cock had their union tickets in order.

"Here you are then," he said, leaning into the Nissen, a worried dark eager face with the button eyes of a marmoset.

"Yes we are then," replied the Old Cock, "for what bleeding good it does us and for what business it is of yours."

"I been meaning to have a bit of a word with you, old man," replied the fellow-worker, "being as I am shop steward here and bearing in mind what a fight we have had in our industry during the past, having got our union where it is today we have to make sure everything is in order although there's nothing personal against you in the matter. I wouldn't want you to think we had it for you personal, but with every tom, dick and harry fiddling into what is reckoned by some to be a cushy old number naturally we have to protect ourself like the capitalist hisself does."

"Enough said," replied the Old Cock, "you have a good case, mate, and you want to stick to it, don't he, Arpie, because things is going to get a bloody sight worse than you might horribly dream of after a welsh rabbit supper. Take us for instance. Here am I, a clean-living, hard-working, skilled man in a profession without which a very fine state of affairs you would be in with the garbage stinking up the entire world, me a public servant of some years' standing with a record second to none even if I say so myself, with I won't discuss what decorations, we don't give a light for all that, although I might point out a serious buttock wound (non-pensionable after ten years) not to mention a slight residue of gas in the gut which passing through has nevertheless left the lower bowel in an irritated condition likely to breed tape-worms and the like intestinal parasites, but forget all that and look at it as a common or garden man in the street who after giving all for his King and Country is now (you will hardly credit the fact) cast aside like an old hat to graze on pastures new if any should be forthcoming, which they won't due to me being temporary grading and therefore fit only for Potter's Field always taking it for granted they have the spare accommodation."

"Did they give you the push?" asked the man.

"They give me the push," replied the Old Cock.

"Belong to a union?" asked the man.

"I always have voted Conservative and I always will," said the Old Cock defiantly. "Leave government to them who is best fitted by their classy education for the filthy job. The working man don't want his own in power because then he's got to spit on hisself, but them other lot, the gents, so long as they got the running of things we know where we are and who is to blame, and a man can be free to hate the bastards in power without them turning out to be second cousins from Birmingham. This council which is giving me the nine-ten-out is a Socialist mob, the thieving upstarts. I been a union man for thirty-six year and a fat lot of good it did me. I got me card here somewhere." He fished out from a reserve pocket of string and dog-ends the already tea-stained letter from Picklewater and a grey grimed woolly union card which did in fact contain some ancient entries of the highway robbery which these Bolshies get away with as the loot for having organized theirselves into the cushiest number outside of mess-serge in a rookie centre.

"What's he?" asked the man, looking at the ever-busy Arp. "Also a scuppered old union man, old man?"

"Me partner," introduced the Old Cock waving his hand in the direction of Arp who quietly straightened nails, cleaning the rust off with second-hand emery-cloth and thinking it will be nice to have a full box of nice shiny nails. "A master tradesman and a very quiet cove. When I am pushed so is he, and if I am shoved so he falls over."

"My advice as a steward and a fellow-man is go and complain to your union, that's my advice," advised the fellow-man.

"I'll bear it in mind, old chap," answered the Old Cock. "When the unions is the masters in our fair land and standing with their boots across our dirty necks I'll think of your advice and what you said. They are all rotten, old chap, take my word for it. Whoever holds the upper hand is

[141]

evil to the under-dog. We want more brothers like dear old Arp here who get on with cleaning up the rusty nails, not big-heads who interfere with your brains, fill up your earoles, nose and throat with a lot of old cod, de-louse you, marry you, hold your hand while you're on the job, buttonhole your nipper so soon as he peeps out his long bald head, dress him in khaki and send him out with a gun so before he catches his packet he will have generously bestowed upon numerous other poor bastards theirs, and all the time our protectors in the councils *and* the unions *and* the governments *and* the cabinets are giving out with a lot of bullshit to the effect we are attacking no one, we are defending freedom. I'll think of you, old chap, when we march on bleeding feet into Berlin again or Armenteers or Timbuktu or the Kremlin herself with little old father Stalin locked up in a madhouse where him and the rest of our polluted masters belong. Because they're all mad, old chap. Listen to me, Arp old fellow, as true as we stand here three normal working men who hope to live, the bosses of all sorts, the leaders, the guvners, our bloody pince-neyed protectors with their public-loving phizzogs and their deep-down private hate-bags, they are the lot of them stone mad, otherwise why would they take the jobs, why want to boss lousy old us about in the first place if they wasn't a bit cracked? They got all the wrong feelings and all the right thoughts, split like rotten taters they are, off their chumps, my friends, loopy, barmy, gone nuts, plain crackers, and the less they do for us the better off we shall be just doing what we feel like for those of us we fancy with everything for everyone, fill your gut, sleep in a bed, fight back together when you're hit, drop dead if you get any big ideas about being the great O'Reilly himself, and to hell with what the loony bosses tell you is your duty."

The Old Cock suddenly ran out of ammunition.

"Do you think the union can do anything?" he muttered, tapping the table with his horny broken finger-nails.

The man tut-tutted back, "My advice is see them, you can lose nothing by seeing them, although if you don't mind my saying so, old man, I don't think your present attitude is exactly progressive and co-operative."

"I don't want progress and co-ops," cried the Old Cock. "I just want me rights or if that's too

[143]

much to ask, what I can get without stooping to the murder of widows, orphans and the crippled of twenty-eight world wars past and future."

After the indignant steward left he turned to Arp, who had already filled a tin Oxo box with shining nails.

"Don't think it weak of me, Arp," he said, shame-faced as a dog caught nosing the meat-dish, "if I do actually pop down to the union office tomorrow. It isn't as if I believed in the swine, just that, well frankly, Arpie, old crow, I just don't know what else an old cock like me can do when he becomes one of the Lord's redundant creatures waiting for the last post to call him home." He held the woolly union card a yard or so from his nose where it dangled like an over-ripe sock-heel. "I'd better just clean this up a bit," he grumbled, "better get everything ship-shape for me ship-mates in the Sanitary and Sewage. Why don't you do the six-inch nails and the rest as well as them four-inchers? You don't like to mix the breeds, do you, Arpie? A funny old tidy mind you got, haven't you?"

In which said mind Arp was now thinking a piece of cardboard cut out to the exact size and laid over the inside top of the Oxo tin will save the damp setting up that damaging rust all over again. The Old Cock is carrying on alarming all day today. Something must be bothering him. What? Who?

I I

Who is this big dog with mangled ears and scarred flanks, his greenish sagging coat a flapping flea-ridden skin, his eyes furtive and yellow, an unthreatening snarl stamped upon his carious mouth, sneaking along the muddy gutters of mean streets, muttering dark threats as children playing hopscotch skirt him and decent house-wives out cut-price shopping cross the street to avoid his evil eye?

The Old Cock, fighting every inch of the sod-den way, ducking down the private trenches of his proud and frightened independence, taking short cut after short cut to try and lose his way, shambling through back-streets to make a sur-prise visit to Union H.Q. which, say what you like, will be staffed by a toffy-nose who makes you queue up with burning cheeks to write on bits of paper wheres and whyfors which are none of his cold-eyed business, only in the end to tell you come back in a week to a fortnight. It made a man a chi-yiking puppy dog, the Old Cock a grievous old mongrel begging for a dry marrow-less knuckle-bone from butchers whose smily faces are a mask for the villainy of being in a position to say no and enjoy it, the pen-pushing snipe

He knew them all right, the sad madmen, give them a woman or a drink or a rump-steak and their queasy tummies rise, but set before them a bloke down on his uppers and their small rat-eyes shine at the chance to organise the guts out of his life. Oh, you weasels and stoats, he thought, his tight lips forming the words (so venomous and powerful was his thinking) you long wriggly furry beasties with pointed teeth all slavering to bite and leave your poisoned spit in a man's heart-flesh. Oh tigers that roam the streets for laughing prey. Oh leopards that spring from the grey slate roof and slaughter in the asphalt road. An orange cat stared with yellow eyes from a broken black-ish cast-iron gate, knowing him an enemy to its predatory ambition to pounce on mice and mangle them.

"Git, you bastard," hissed the Old Cock, and

dashed his fist at the murdering critter. But they was cunning itself. The orange cat leapt from the fence and the fist struck iron, the ball of its thumb bruising and a little blood beading up as the Old Cock brought the damaged part to his mouth to suck.

Now he turned in his tracks, his disgusted back to their dirty underhand tricks. Why let their orange cats threaten him, their cast-iron break his hands? Why play their game, you can't win, the man in the street can't win, he is out-classed, baffled, bogged-down in the mud-flats waiting for the enemy to send up his rockets and flares and come over, step by step, the saw-edges of his bayonets dull glinting under the grease, his staring yellow eyes watching your every move, the saliva in his mouth waiting to run as after the war-scream, the knife sprang, struck, tore in and turned in your belly.

He stopped by a poster of a happy face which was saying, "I saved for a rainy day," pressed his hands to his stomach and admitted that the tape-worm was fear. He stood pale, the words streaming out of mind like blood getting lost in the soupy mud. With his lips quite still he wished with all the year-beaten regret of his panicky heart that he was not he but Arp to be silent and daft and unafraid. He closed his eyes and rested against the poster on the wall and his days washed over him. There was a sharp pain under his left breast, and he was grateful to have it to hold on to.

The Old Cock stood there, the unknown old soldier, waiting for yet another bombardment to pass, while the rubbish washed on a high tide of blood from a brain which, to be frank, was somewhat confused. For nothing is simple. Put it this way, if Bates was bashed on the nut and the nut cracked out will only pop another Bates; if he is bashed on the nut and that nut cracked out will pop yet another Bates; and so on until you have a whole council of them moving down on you with claws of varying sizes all keen to score you out of the running for ever and ever. But then it wasn't Bates, not him we all know and hate but him behind the back of him (what's his name?) who plays the tune (scraggy bird in an art-gilded cage) till his swinish fancy tires and you are whipped into the cold, cold snow (what was his perishing name? something like Pickle-water).

Cutting the cackle, it's a bloody washout in

which the baby is thrown out with the bathwater and devil take all. Talk about Rights. What Rights? Then I will tell you (shouts the on-parade voice in the Old Cock's battered braincase) the right of an Englishman true-born and free to get his beer and baccy, his java, bread and scrape, plum-and-apple, cut off the joint and choice of two veg, his kip, his oats, his noggin and his nooky, good things sent in plenty from heaven above but niggled into pigeon-holes by charity charlies with scrag-end notions of that arithmetical dead loss and bad debt Man (for which abstraction please substitute the Old Cock and read on regardless).

There's nothing like getting really airyated and blowing one's top for putting the kybosh on squawking miseries, getting your guts back, and setting you up proud as a peacock to spit in the eye of all and sundry who are plotting your downfall. After a really good ding-dong you are all limbered up and ready to roar, so watch out all you council-employed cats and union-serving villains, here comes the wanky old avenger with the sure knowledge that right is might and two pints in his rattling darby-kelly to prove it. For to put it baldly, the Old Cock soon after his moment of truth dropped into the nearby Merry Fiddlers for a quick one (it being, conveniently, opening time).

In the short respite he becomes, once again, his own man, all heart-beating hushed, all panic past, and a little before their midday knocking-off time arrives at the local headquarters of that tribute to the solidarity of the working class, the Sanitary, Sewage and General Workers Union, a grubby paint-flaking shop-front with blacked-out windows, a smell of kerosene stoves, carbolic soap, and Woodbines starting the nose off on the right foot as the glass-fronted door creaks open (postered "Labour is *your* Party" in a Co-op print job to make you proud). Walk in, brother, and shout for the hippo in charge.

"No good you shouting, mate," said a thin fellow in an ex-army great-coat dyed navy blue, a white silk choker and a grey homburg with a yellow stain all round its black band, rolling a thin mixture of black shag and dog-ends in a Rizla cigarette paper. "They ain't finished counting the dues that come in this morning yet. Here, Horace," he called through the glass ticket-office partition, "there's a gentleman to see you. It's a pleasure to sniff your breath," he went on. "I'm only waiting for the boozers to close so I won't be tempted to do in the old sickness benefit. I got a black patch on me left lung the size of a ten-pound note, though it goes without saying it don't reckon that kind of money."

The Old Cock tore the poster off the door.

"They told us to bloody unite," he shouted, "and now they don't want to know."

"I'll say toodloo then," said the thin man smiling. Sickly thinking it don't do you no good to be seen with these Bolshie or IRA blokes he ducked out into the street.

"Give us this day our daily bread," bellowed the Old Cock, "or give us some service instead."

A young fellow with brilliantine hair, a clean collar, a red tie and a tweed suit, smoking a cherry-wood pipe, came out, told him to take it easy, showed him into an office with a worn bit of carpet in front of a burbling gas fire, and offered him a fag from a tobacco tin.

"Fight, you bastard," said the Old Cock, "why don't you stand up and fight like a man?"

But because the young fellow wouldn't but only sent into an adjoining gaff for a cup of tea which he paid for out of his own pocket, the Old Cock wanted to bawl. Instead he blew his nose into one of the bits of rag Arp had stitched into hankies for them, and told all.

"It's all this Bates," he started, "not just him but his boss, Picklewater or something like that his rotten name is . . ."

Boyle, the decent young union-man, checked his cards, made notes and did some arithmetic, finding that the council owed the Old Cock for more than nine years' overtime. Boyle reckoned the figure conservatively to be in the region of eight hundred pound, on account of which claim the Union might be prepared to advance a loan not exceeding twenty-five pound cash.

The Old Cock couldn't have been out cold for more than five minutes, but it was long enough to fight through the whole Battle of Mons again with the shells whining and screaming and the earth thudding in giant black snowballs and the mud raining and the stray bullets snicking through the dark and sometimes finding a home in a head upraised for a moment too long. He fought the battle through, every nerve-jump and heart-beat, the smells of fear and failure all fused into one mouldy smell by the heat of battle. He thought of the column-jumping and lead-swinging Bateses back a hundred miles away at

[153]

the base wearing their bare-arsed medals and waiting for the victory parade and hoped that a special big shell spewed out of the belly of the biggest bloody Bertha in the world was sailing over looking for them. He waited with his bowels tense wishing he'd had one more meal, and one more drink, and one more smoke, and one more bash at the Red Light, and swearing that if he came through that's what he'd do for ever after. When the bombardment stopped he looked around to see who was dead beside him in the trench because someone was and there was this fellow saying, "Take a drink of tea, take a little sip of tea, old cock, it'll do you good."

"I thought we'd copped it," the Old Cock whispered as he took the cup-edge between his lips. He drank, then pushed the cup away. "How much did you say? No don't tell me. I might go off again. Do you think they'll shell out?"

"They might argue," the young fellow said, "but they'll have to fork out something in the end."

"In the end?" repeated the Old Cock getting shakily to his feet. "Sod the end. I'm going straight over to the council office and spit in their thieving eye, the lead-swinging trench rats."

But he had to wait ten minutes all the same because his legs were a couple of jellied eels, and his heart was beating like a chicken trying to get out of its shell.

12

I<small>T'S</small> <small>NO</small> <small>GOOD</small> anyone saying that the Old Cock
was a pernickity old so-and-so who should have
gone through the proper channels, because he
did look high and low round the council offices
for a proper channel without success. There
wasn't one in the surveyor's department only the
usual snotties in sports-jackets and brilliantine,
and an elderly clerk with a bald-head and a pipe-
cleaner in his hand though no pipe, who when he
heard the Old Cock's business said to try other
channels further down the passage but on the
floor below.

So the Old Cock tried further down the passage on the floor below, which was indeed the
treasurer's department but you could see the
skinny crab-lice didn't have two halfpennies
to rub together, let alone his eight hundred stolen

nicker. So he went down again to the hall where the commissionaire walked back and forth waiting for his bowels to ease after his canteen dinner of two helpings of pie and chips followed by two of spotted dick with treacle.

"Here, corp," the Old Cock called.

"Sergeant — and not so loud," replied the ex-corporal.

"Where do I go for claims?" asked the Old Cock very civil.

"Claims for what?" asked the other.

"Mind your own bloody business," answered the Old Cock, "you bleeding supply-corps cookhouse wallah."

"Out," ordered the official, catching the Old Cock's coat copper-style and helping him down the steps without any trouble at all. "Come back when you learn some manners."

"I'll have you out of that job," the Old Cock shouted from the bottom step. "You just laid hands on someone who is a shareholder in your uniform, you horrible berk." The commissionaire looked straight through him to a bowler-hatted merchant in a Montague Burton natty suiting, and saluted. Which hurt the Old Cock's feelings more than anything, because if we have to take to wearing bowlers before we can get a bit of simple co-operation from our fellow-man who shall not be spat on from a mighty height?

He turned to go mumbling, "I come to them full of trust and good faith, laying it on the line straight and fair, a tired old gentleman all alone in this cruel world of bowler-hatted bean-eyed bed-bugs, with no place to rest me weary head, yet I am worth a fortune in over-time if they give me what is rightfully mine by the sweat of me brow and the white hairs sprouting on me ancient dome. By why wear it? Why bow down to their bullying? I won't wear it. Why should I?" And he turned back to the steps.

But there was the commissionaire waiting with his big arms and his glassy face not missing a move the Old Cock made, just like the police all over, begging you to hang one on them so they can pull you in for grievous bodily harm.

"Don't stand there like a tit in a trance," he shouted at the officer. "Come round the back and roll your sleeves up, you coward." He mooched round the back and waited, fists clenched, edgy as a bitch on heat.

"You can't talk," the Old Cock told himself, "to a bloke who looks straight through you with

[158   ]

glass eyes like a kewpie-doll. If you talk to yourself it sends you barmy. What an unfortunate
caper it all is. Dear, oh dear, oh bless my soul, oh
crumbs, oh golly, oh lawks, oh bligh, oh blink.
I'm going to keep in the position of defence without losing me temper and without proper swearing once. Starting from now. Now. Oh gord,
oh Christ (that's not swearing that's someone's
name), oh blind, oh dickory, oh dockery, oh
sausage, oh pease pud, oh faggot, oh bollick
(watch it), oh crumpet, crumpet isn't real swearing because it don't have to mean under, oh
muffin could be just as rude for anybody with a
dirty mind. Oh sugar, oh shit, that was a slip of
the tongue, you can't count that. Oh piggy, oh
poggy, oh doggy, oh pussy. I hate animals, specially cats, ginger cats, stinking around the place.
Where is that bloody bullying sergeant, damn his
eyes. What the bleeding sodding buggering bastard hell am I doing with myself, hopping around
like a fart on a curtain-pole waiting for someone
to get me out of trouble? Gord's bleeding life, if
I was someone else I wouldn't piss on me." He
saw an entrance down some steps and charged
into it shouting, "Down with toadying arse-
kissers and lousy boot-lickers."

"Not too much noise, mate, if you don't mind," said a thin, sandy-haired fellow lying on his stomach by the boilers. "I think I'm on to something now."

"Beg your pardon," the Old Cock said quietly when he saw what the ginger-nut was up to. "It's a skilled trade rat-catching, ain't it? After the master-hole?"

"Yes," said the ginger-nut. "I know it's down here somewhere in the footings of the boilers where it's nice and warm. Your typical rat hugs his comfort. They come back year after year to the same hole."

"Ever hear of a ghost rat?" the Old Cock asked. "Bloke I knew turn round and see a big rat black as Newgate's knocker with red eyes staring him straight in the face from a shell-hole, and wherever he was posted he see that very same black rat till he copped his lot one morning from a sniper and that same bloody black rat was perched stone dead on his head when the stretcher-bearers picked him up. We reckoned it was a ghost rat and all the rats in the trenches was one each for all the different blokes. There goes one, a brown big one."

"Female," said the rat-catcher. "We don't

want to knock all the females over or there won't be much use left for the profession, will there?"

"Ever use ferrets?"

"I do sometimes," the rat-catcher said, "because your ferret will get your rat out and I reckon it's unhealthy to have all them dead vermin rotting under the floors and walls. But the ferret is nearly a thing of the past now. The young fellows won't take the trouble to train them up."

"Like everything else," sighed the Old Cock, "it's all going to pot in the trades."

"The thing of it is," explained the rat-catcher, "the kitchens up above brings them back. While you get the kitchens right on top of all the piping from the boilers it is ideal breeding ground, and knocking the rats down every couple of year ain't no use. Do you know how many offspring your average couple of rats put out in a year?"

"Highly profilic," said the Old Cock. "Is the kitchens up there then?"

"Straight up the stone stairs," said the rat-catcher plugging a hole and grunting.

"Thanks, mate," replied the Old Cock.

[161   ]

At the top of the stone stairs outside a pair of glass swing doors labelled *No Admittance* were three dustbins containing a fortune in stale loaves. "No excuse for that for a start," the Old Cock said. "Make a lovely bread pudden with a few raisins and sultanas, you can't beat a real good bread pudden. Let's have a dekko." He pushed the doors slightly apart and squinted through. "What's this?" he whispered amazed. "I'd know that bottom anywhere. Mrs. Goffin," he called softly, "here, madam."

She looked up with a look of who's that knocking at my door. "Why it's Barnacle Bill the Sailor," she said, looking round to make sure no one was about. "Stay there," she said, "it's no admittance to gentlemen callers." She slunk between the doors. "They'll have my life if they know I'm getting stage-door Johnnies round the kitchen. I suppose they give you the push from the studio as well, did they?"

"I resigned," the Old Cock said, "they owe me a lot of money and they won't pay up so I just handed in me note of resignation."

"They put us all back over here," said Mrs. Goffin. "Pity really because I think that filming's ever so interesting, especially after cooking

[162   ]

here month after month feeding the civil service. It was too good to last, I suppose. I hear that
Mr. Corst bank-ruptured hisself and the council
is furious at the loss."

"So they should be," said the Old Cock. "One
or two of the boys round the studio never had
much faith in that Fred Karno outfit."

"They come out nigh-on as fast as they come
in," said Mrs. Goffin. "I've sort of lost touch over
here. Can't lay me hands on a single thing —
unlike some I could mention."

"Meaning?" asked the Old Cock, sidling round
her.

"That Mr. Bates was in for breakfast."

"Was he?"

"Yes. He said I wouldn't be troubled by you
again."

"Did he?"

"Yes. He was ever so kind over at the studios.
But I never liked his type much."

"Didn't you?"

"No. Did he get you the push because of that
bit of argee-bargee that day?"

"Give us a kiss then."

"No."

"Go on, Emily."

[163   ]

"No. Hurry up then if you must."

The Old Cock gave her a big sploshy one on the cheek. "Gives me an appetite," he said.

"I got some cold bangers left over from their breakfast," she replied, pink as bun-icing.

"Give us a couple and come down the boozer with us tonight."

"Which one?"

"The Merry Fiddlers."

"What time?"

"Seven o'clock."

"I must run."

The Old Cock was half-way down the stone stairs when she called him back. "Don't you want your bangers then, you soppy old fossil?"

Wait till Arp hears this, the Old Cock thought as he galloped down the stairs swallowing mouthfuls of cold pork sausage, it's an ill-wind blows nobody any good, who would have thought in the very strong-hold of the enemy to have found a friend and ally. Because I want to think of her in that way, straight I do, as a friend from whom I can get a bit of comfort — nothing detrimental, just good friends that's all, and if it leads on to something more serious, well, I'm in a position to keep her in the style she should be kept

[164]

in. I'll just say to her, Emily, me eight hundred quid is in the Post Office, I'm in fair wind, in fact good shape so long as I keep me blood-pressure down and don't give the old tum a chance to play up. What about it?

"You should have been here just now," the ginger rat-catcher said, "bloody great dog-rat the size of a horse got his teeth stuck in me thumb. Look at the blood he drew," he went on proudly waving a red-soaked hankie. "Seems a pity to kill a great dog that big. You never know when you'll see another like it."

"Their fangs poison?" asked the Old Cock.

"Not to me," answered the rat-catcher. "I'm scarred all over me hands. Look."

"Yes you are. Cheero," said the Old Cock.

"Cheero," answered the rat-catcher. "Did you clear up your trouble what you was swearing about when you come in?"

"More or less," answered the Old Cock. "I got the union looking out for me."

"They definitely get up your nose these council pen-pushers," the rat-catcher stated.

"Yes they definitely do," said the Old Cock. "Cheero."

"Cheero," said the rat-catcher.

Down at union building young Boyle was in the middle of a ding-dong by telephone.

"No good you saying, old man," he told the telephone, "that he never clocked in for overtime. The question is do you admit or do you not the fact that a watchman can't watch days and nights without doing overtime. Sit down," he whispered to the Old Cock. "They've already admitted a degree of liability."

"Give it to the scum good and proper," encouraged the Old Cock hoarsely. "Never mind about degree."

"All very well, old man," Boyle continued, "if there was a clock for him to clock in by at the place of work. Yes, old man, I do know what I'm talking about. No, I'm not rattled. Yes. You do that, old man." He replaced the receiver. "He doesn't have a leg to stand on," Boyle said lighting up his old cherrywood. "What's your problem now?"

"I was just thinking," said the Old Cock chewing his moustache.

"Oh yes?" said Boyle. "Of course all that business he's making over the clocking-in is bloody nonsense in this case."

"No question," replied the Old Cock, "it's just

[166   ]

their little minds the way they want everything writ down, don't matter if it's right under their very nose they don't believe it. The thing is though I was just thinking."

"What?" Boyle asked, putting another match to his cherrywood.

"That needs a good pull-through," the Old Cock said. "It's all bunged up with nickeltine."

"Run out of cleaners. That's the curse of pipe-smoking."

"Funny you should say that," said the Old Cock, "because this morning I see a bloke down at the town hall had a bloody handful of cleaners but no pipe. No — what I was thinking was about this here claim of mine."

"Yes?" said Boyle, poking the stem of the pipe with a match-stick which broke.

"This claim," the Old Cock went on, "how would it be if we pitched it a bit lower? I mean eight hundred nicker. It's too much."

"On actual time it actually comes out to seven hundred and sixty-eight pounds, seventeen shillings and fourpence, less tax."

"Yes, they'll want their bloody money, no doubt," agreed the Old Cock. "Maybe if we sort of came down a bit we'd get round 'em easier."

"Why the hell should we?" asked Boyle. "I don't understand the working man. First he wants his rights, then he gets the wind-up."

"There's no call to talk to me that way," said the Old Cock. "I always been one to stand up for me rights and I always will. No — it's just that I was just thinking, that's all, sort of all round the question."

"There's no call to turn your back on what is rightfully yours. Time enough when they make an offer to think of settling, to save court costs and that kind of thing, not before. That got it," Boyle added as a great piece of black tobacco came out of the pipe.

"What I was thinking would be nice," said the Old Cock, pushing his moustache up and down, "would be if you was to let me have a bit of that few quid you said the union might loan me on account of me claim. For running expenses like."

"Why didn't you say so?" replied Boyle, finally getting his pipe lit. "You can have it out of the special-purposes fund."

"You know how it is," the Old Cock said, "you don't like to ask. A few quid'll do to carry us over."

"You can have the whole twenty-five," Boyle

said, his chin jutting out. "The bloody union'll have to follow the case up if they've actually got money involved."

"You shouldn't talk like that about the union," said the Old Cock, as he took the money. "I haven't had a bundle like this since the missus was in the local slate-club. Our Christmas share come up to thirty-two pound. The bastard secretary made off with the whole lot the very next year but she was dead so I wasn't myself involved."

"Look after it now," said Boyle, "because they're going to scream blue murder when they hear. I'm really riled over this case."

"I'm a highly providential type of fellow," the Old Cock replied, putting the money in his back trouser-pocket.

"I think I'll give the town hall another call," Boyle replied, reaching for the telephone suddenly worried whether he had gone a bit far. "This case really has me riled."

"See you another time, then," the Old Cock said, and beetled out and up the road hell for leather, thinking he looks like he might change his mind so let's get temptation out of his way before.

In order to make speed without becoming too

much of a side-show, the Old Cock put on that he was a long-distance walker in training like you see them going round the block sometimes, their bony behinds twisting side to side like clock pendulums and their peanut legs trotting up and down like liberty horses. He took to the gutter and raising his bent arms high made a record half-mile before puffed to the world he had to sit down to get his wind back.

Almost straight away a hot flush came over him, part from the exertion and part from (naturally) just having come into money. He gave a moment's thought to the ways of this crummy old ball of clay on which we sit puffing and grunting and blowing waiting for the end and all the while between not knowing whatever next. How first the lords taketh everything away for no reason hardly, how next they give everything back for equally no reason hardly. How it is all a game of rummy, certainly a rummy old game, with beanfeasts for the winners and kicks up the backsides for the soppy old loser, a battlefield it is, he thought, with no Queensbury rules, beggar your neighbour, punch under the belt when the ref's back is turned, fight the good fight with all thy might, thou band of Christian brothers, (as the old padre who stopped a stray one used to whisper in your earole as he passed up and down the trench, at least he come under fire, not like some of the dog-collar brigade).

A man in a homburg hat with an umbrella who certainly should have known better, passed by, and ignoring the Old Cock hunched up with his legs under him and his back against the wall, let fly a real solid gob which whizzed past the resting nose like an iron fist, going smack-bang through the grating of the gutter-drain. I never in all my years, thought the Old Cock, see a gent in a homburg hat spit in the street with such force and accuracy. Like I was saying, you never know what you will see next. The world is wonderful in the morning, as the old song has it.

Greatly encouraged by a day so full of interesting developments happening in the nick of time, the Old Cock, one hand on his heart and the other picking his ear, strolled down the street, eyes wide with wonder, wondering what to do between now and opening time. For already the money was hot as a mustard-plaster just below the small of his back, slowly burning a hole in his pocket.

13

BUT WHAT, if you don't mind the question, do you want with such a thing? What good is it? Can you wear it — no. Can you cut off a slice to eat with a glass of tea — no." Rambam squinted his eyes at the bright face of the Old Cock. "Anyway, not to put too fine a point on it, you look plain ridiculous in a helmet, like Sir Sprawncelot after he was drowned in the lake. Take it off. You don't know where it's been."

The Old Cock pulled the vizor of the helmet down and said in a muffled voice, "Do you or do you not want to sell it?" He lifted the vizor. "Do you sell gear to the passing public from your emporium or do you not? What do you have things in the shop for if every time a client asks how much a thing is you have to give them an argument? Call yourself a business man? How much for the bloody old suit of armour?"

Rambam picked up a grieve or a curiasse or whatever the hell they're called, and dropped it back in the box with a clank. "What good can it do you? Save your money. It cost me four pound ten. What can I charge you?" he said shaking his head.

The Old Cock sorted out a kind of big iron glove affair and dragged it on to his left hand. "You feel real safe in a uniform like this," he said. "I can understand how them knights of old was so full of brag and bull, standing up there with half-a-ton of gas-stove between them and the hun. Where's the gallant old sword?"

"For four pound ten," Rambam replied, "I didn't get a sword. Only the armour itself. The sword was a separate lot which I didn't fancy running to."

"You should have got the complete set," the Old Cock advised, "penny wise pound foolish. How much for the lot as it stands then, and don't give me arguments, just the price, take it or leave it." He pulled the helmet off. "I reckon one of the Boer War bayonets, or maybe something a bit earlier, Waterloo stuff maybe, might fit in quite well with this lot. I see a very old bayonet some- where? Where was it? Well, don't hang me up

[173   ]

all night long while you're chewing your gums. I have a previous engagement of a delicate nature. I needn't say more to a man of the world like yourself."

"Cherching for femms still at your age? It's neither nice nor suitable. I'll take six pound for the armour but it's an academy question because from where do you get six pound?" Rambam bent down to push the box back under a table.

"Not so fast," said the Old Cock, putting his still-gloved hand on Rambam's shoulder.

"It weighs a ton that thing," Rambam said. "There's a fortune in metal in such a thing."

The Old Cock reached his bundle of green ones out of his back trouser-pocket and waved them to cool off. "I have just come into money," he said, "ask no questions and you'll hear no lies."

"Stolen? You done a bit of a job somewhere? In this case I don't think I can sell. Furthermore, it's not my business, but I must say I am surprised and ashamed to ever give such a think a thought." Rambam was upset and his plummy eyes darted away from the Old Cock and downwards.

"Don't be insulting," the Old Cock said, very put out. "I admit I done a fair bit of scrounging in me time, what you can scrounge it being general admitted is the perks of any job, but hold hard on the stealing caper if you don't mind. I hardly stole a thing me entire life. You don't want to be insulting, mate, you won't ever rise in the business world if you start taking liberties with the public in that way."

"Six pound," said Rambam, a bit rattled. "I can't take less and I still say you are what someone might call up the pole to even buy such a thing. But you tell me to mind my own business so I'm minding it. Six pound."

The Old Cock gave him the notes with a flourish, then added half-a-crown. "Get some deserving youngster to hump it over to the old shlosh or castle. No hard feelings, I trust?"

"No harm meant, none taken, I'm sure," Rambam replied, all smiles again. "After all, lords and ladies pay hundreds to stick such junk in their marble halls so why not you?"

"I may make a whole collection of old-time fighting gear," the Old Cock said, "when me estate is settled. I'll have you scouting round for it, Rambam, on a commission basis."

"I never touch that commission basis," Rambam said. "I buy for myself and sell for myself the old-fashioned way."

[175]

"Never mind," the Old Cock replied, "we'll come to a suitable arrangement. I'll just take this old glove with me in case I'm set on by cats or other treacherous animals. Toodloo."

Farewell, I should have said, the Old Cock thought, as Rambam touched his forelock in salute, a sloppy one but the old fellow didn't have the proper training. Lift the right arm in a parallel to the seam of your trousers to ninety degrees bringing the forearm up to the forehead making an angle of forty-five degrees. Salute hipe. Present hipe. What was hipe? Hipe was the blanco, bullshit, spit and polish, which made the British Army the unconquerable mob of veteran contemptibles they were.

> *We are Kitchener's Army*
> *The Army of the free*
> *We cannot shoot, we cannot fight*
> *What bloody use are we?*

"Kitchener wants you," the Old Cock went on out loud. "He's about the only bastard what does." If you didn't jump to it when he pointed, you would have more white feathers growing out of your backside than a prize pullet. All those bleeding busybodies who couldn't wait to make a hero out of you, although fair's fair, we were a bit in a hurry ourself, what with the singing and dancing and the big sploshy kisses from the posh girls you got the idea it was a party going on over there, over there, over there, not dig your own grave and sit in it. I bet no brass-hat ever planned that all that buckshee earth was going to run back under our feet as oozy, soupy mud, till we was all like pilchards canned in the trenches in thick tomato sauce, up to the earoles in sweet violets. Then the old taters in the mould set in and your feet froze solid black till stink, nothing stinks like a pair of dead plates of meat.

"What you wearing that for, mate?" a pug-nosed boy about fourteen and runtish shouted from a fish-monger's delivery bike loaded with the Old Cock's newly acquired armour.

The Old Cock pulled the gauntlet on tighter and held it up clenched in a knightly farewell.

"Farewell, page," he said. "Sling your bloody hook and complete your mission."

"Crackers," said the boy, and peddled off.

The Old Cock looked after him for a moment, a warm smile about his lips, a tear starting to his eye.

"Pray gord he gets through the enemy lines.

[177]

Gord bless his trusty steed. I'll mention them both in dispatches for this."

In days of old when knights were bold and paper wasn't invented, a man could look a soldier with a horse under his backside and never worry so long as he kept up there. A horse was what you needed with your good old suit of armour, a jolly old gee gee, carthorse strong, none of your flighty light-weight Epsom fillies.

The horses never did get much of a recommendation again after that ancient time, the new-fangled shrapnel tending to cut off their legs, but they made good eating, a bit sweetish but good while they lasted at the front those first few months, after which the soldiers in scarlet on the pretty dancing nags from Pall Mall got soaked in mud and come out no fancier than the Old Cock or Taffy or Soldier Gribble who wore the same puttees without delousing for seventeen weeks, a record even in the British Army. Soldier reckoned he was immune to lice by bad blood through loose living, but you should have seen them puttees when prised off to reveal a mild gangrene case for which he was bunged on a charge, taking your puttees off every so often being a standing order for health reasons, though what good your health was to you in this poxing mob would someone please tell us. They called him Soldier because he hated it, being by profession, he always proudly lied, a horse-thief working in Erin's green and horsey land, and certainly he had a bit of a brogue and was a great whipper-up of odds and sods which anyone had left lying around.

"Dirty bastard he was too," the Old Cock mumbled. "Dirtier than meself. But you would have called him a prince on horseback." As they was forced to agree that night when they all tanked up on cognac down at the estaminay or local, the good old Virgin of Nantes, where they sorted theirself out three willing virgins and was going great guns, the old mum in the corner knitting away and chewing her gums meanwhile, when they look round and see Soldier has done a bunk. So they take it in turns with his filly, the Old Cock observing they was all bare-bloody-back riders that night. Then suddenly in busts Soldier. He drags them off their lady-loves and over to the door. There all on the same bit of rope are three bloody great white cart-horses shining patiently in the moonlight. "Now admit I'm a genuine horse-thief," he shouts, "or I'll black your eyes."

Laughing and joking they jump on the horses, the three of them shoving and pushing, Taffy heaving himself on by the tail, the Old Cock pulling on the mane of his, and off they gallop up the moonlit road, past the shelled skeleton houses, the three virgins of Nantes screaming after them, the old mum dropping her stitches from shock because they haven't paid, the whore-thieving horse-thieves.

"They shall not pass Verdun," shout the three dirty beggars on horseback. "Up Foch. Up Kitchener. Up Fred Karno."

They reckoned they was taking the road back home and you could knock them down with a white feather when they come round the next morning with the three white horses disappeared like a willing girl in a dream and the shells crunching over their heads into the allied trenches which they had over-reached, the three shadowy horsemen left far behind the lines laughing their way Blightywards through the grey fields, but the three of them, poor bastards, back in the bog again.

Pity they didn't issue armour and horses to the poor bloody infantry. They would have looked better and been better protection too against the bricks the old bags chucked not to mention the more damaging showers hurled by enemy howitzers. "I ought to get an old nag," the Old Cock said aloud, "when me money comes through. Maybe a bit of an old cart-horse so as me and Arp can travel the country in the rag-and-bone business on our own account. We might call the horse Fred Karno in memory of that other gallant steed. I wonder where is the best place to buy a white cart-horse cheap?"

There's a fortune in the old rag-and-bone lark, all you need is a bit of capital, and that's what he had all right, the good old bit of essential capital.

"As I walk along the bwudibelong with a hindependent hair," the Old Cock hummed, "you can hear the girls declaire I must be a millionaire." And I could be too, he thought, I could make a pack of dibs, so if she turned me down La Goffin would be real sorry later on when she read it in the *Daily Mirror* how I hit it rich in the old metal. Well, good fortune has taken its time to sort me out but the advantage of being a mature man before you come into your lot is that you know how to handle the loot.

So the Old Cock lolloped on considering the well-worn truth of what an amazing difference a few bob can make to our whole outlook on what, for want of a better name or ever having known better we needs must call LIFE. It is the jimmy o'goblins, the shekels, the sounding brass which alone can give us those capital letters to spell the tired word. *Sans* them we flounder, flake out, and rather contemptible not to say downright sad, crawl to our holes till the dark dustman calls in his fiery horse-drawn corporation cart to carry us off to that bourne from which no old soldier returns. Rather a lovely phrase that, to conceal our loathing for the rubbish dump end, less clearly in sight when rustling green-backs rustle and gleaming silver cart-wheels joyfully clink in our grimy ears.

What better opportunity shall we have to ask ourselves the time-worn unanswerable, "What is Life?" than now as we witness a transformation scene not less miraculous than in the last act of any pantomime? The dingy has fallen away and where before there limped a sagging old ditty-bag of tired nerve-ends, now marches onward ever onward, a few nicker in his pocket, a gallant gauntlet on his hand, his nose in the air, his eyes bright, his wispy moustache streaming to the wind like the mane of a stallion escaped from the

back-yard of a horse-meat purveyor, this somewhat senile attempt to procreate spiritual imper-
fectability, this miraculous anomaly of dung and
dust in (if we may believe what we tell ourself)
God's image, presented not for the first or last
time on the mighty revolving stage and with all
possible vigour musterable on a twenty-five
pound advance, the one and only Old Cock, running like a hoary old wildebeeste over the asphalt
veldt to the Merry Fiddlers, there, proud man, to
make his tiny splash before the inevitable sinking.

14

THE OLD COCK, a-hoop with success and buoyant from the few hot quid in his pocket, floated in to the Saloon of the Merry Fiddlers, wearing his knights-of-old gauntlet as a casual favour to invite inquiries and attract general attention. But so much for the hopes and plans of rats and men, the only wee sleekit beastie in the nest consists of the shebeen's landlord, a jolly publican known to regulars as Tosher, B. I. Metcalfe (with an *e*) licensed to sell alcoholic beverages on and off the premises, tobaccos, wines, and a free house for beers, thus being in a position to please all, from your Stingo merchant to your delicate sippers of blue ruin, port and lemon bibbers, rum and orange sloshers, whisky tipplers, brandy bashers, or Merrydown cider slashers, come one come all to the shiny big fat welcoming ruby-red boozer's boko on dear old Tosher flashing out its strawberry as often as our stupid licensing hours will allow. Tosher, a solid bottled light ale man himself, spiced by a good old whisky every fourth, a rumbling pot-bellied Englishman whose highly fresh complexion could barely contain its disapproval for imported boudoir tipples, a man's man who once being asked for a dry martini showed his ham-fist and the open door to the pouffy inquirer, one who held out against the red rexine and chromium tartiness which is the ruin of our ancient houses, a great polisher of old Spanish mahogany, which, shining like bulls-blood below the deeply bevelled mirrors with their acid-etched trumpet lilies, curlicues and sheaves of barley, proved to the most casual pub-crawler that Tosher kept a house of the old school.

"Evening, Tosher," said the Old Cock, looking round at the empty saloon. "Anyone in the Public?" He let his gauntlet dangle attractively.

"Bit early," replied Tosher. "I hope the necessity don't arise to chuck you out again tonight. I hate that kind of thing."

"Least said soonest mended," said the Old Cock. "It can happen to the best of us, specially on a empty stomach like mine was the last occasion. Like the glove?"

"Bit ropy," said Tosher. "What you wearing one bleeding glove for? What'll it be?"

"Pint of mixed," replied the Old Cock. "Care to examine it a bit closer?" He whipped the glove off in a cavalier gesture and slid it down the bar. "I'll be glad of your opinion."

Tosher served him the pint, then picked up the glove and started to work the jointed metal finger-guards. "Interesting old relic," he remarked. "Old Round Table job I would say, can't tell if it's genuine though."

"Have one yourself," the Old Cock said casually, putting the glove back on his tankard hand, which, though not the right one for it, sort of looked good against the old pewter Tosher sported for regulars.

"You're real flash tonight," Tosher replied. "Bottled ale for me. Win a football pool?"

The Old Cock gave him a straight look, then drained a third of his pint in one. He put the tankard down carefully, wiped his moustache on his sleeve, looked to either side and behind, then pushed his head over the bar and whispered, "On to a very good thing. Can't be more definite just now, but take my word, very good thing for everyone if it comes off. The Government's thinking of taking it up. Bring me a personal fortune, and make all the difference in the event of another world war. Can't say more — but it has to do with Defence of the Realm. I was always keen on that kind of thing."

Tosher looked at him with pitying contempt. "You really are," he said, a little admiration creeping into his tone, "you really are the biggest bloody liar I ever come across in my life."

The Old Cock blinked three times. "Yes, I am," he agreed. "I don't know how I think of 'em meself. They just come into me head."

Tosher shook his head. "It's a sort of gift I suppose," he said.

"I suppose it is," the Old Cock said, "but one thing I have got is a suit of armour, and if you take my advice you'll get one too. We're all going to need them soon."

Tosher looked round the walls of the saloon. "Few bits of gear wouldn't at all look bad," he said. "Picks up the dust though. Mrs. M. wouldn't be too keen on that. What's yours, sir?" he added as a slim fellow, yellow in the face with big brown eyes, came up to the bar.

"A lemon shandy," the man said, "a half." He had a small wooden cage in each hand, each dangling from a string handle. He put them gently down, one on the bar, the other on the floor, as Tosher drew his drink. "Don't want them to see each other yet," he explained to the Old Cock.

"What is he?" the Old Cock asked, peering through the wicket at the little bird inside. "Got a blue beak."

"Linnet," replied the yellow-faced man, "pair of cock linnet."

The Old Cock removed the gauntlet and put it back in his pocket. "Go on," he said. "Our Sunday-school teacher used to keep a cock linnet in a very expensive cage, spoilt it with groundsel and all manner of luscious seed, but would it sing? It never opened his beak except to eat. She kept it in the school room itself, a tin shack back of the chapel it was, because no pets was allowed in her lodgings. We used to pipe up 'Onward Christian Soldiers' warbling away fit to bust to set a good example, but the bleeding bird just looked miserable straight at her. Miss Evelyn Waite she was called, about forty, and no one could ever spell her name right, some made it Wait and some Weight, you can imagine since she weighed in a good sixteen stone she had no luck. She looked at the bird the whole time we was singing, sort of hopeful, I suppose, he would suddenly give out with a trill or two. Years later I come round to seeing the use of Sunday school, one Sunday afternoon when our brats skipped it for some lie or other, and I says to the missus how about a piece in front of the fire and she says are you barmy, the kids aren't at Sunday school. Do yours sing?"

"That's very interesting what you was just saying," the yellow-faced man said.

"What is?" asked the Old Cock.

"That about that cock linnet you had that never would sing."

"That was Miss Waite or Weight, not me."

"Yes, but it's very interesting because they sometimes don't much," insisted the man.

"Don't much what?" asked the Old Cock, a bit edgy.

"Sing," said the man.

"I know they don't," answered the Old Cock. "Isn't that what I just bloody-well went to a lot of trouble to make crystal clear enough, I should have thought, to anybody except a prize bloody village idiot?"

"Don't get airyated, Old Cock," Tosher Metcalfe called from the public bar. "We can hear you out here."

"Here's some bloody fool trying to insult me old Sunday school teacher," shouted the Old Cock.

"No, no, no," persisted the yellow-faced linnet-fancier, "I am saying purely about the linnet, that's all. How they do not sing much if kept in solitary. It is a fact of natural history, that's all I was saying." He gulped the rest of his mare-stale shandy. Pale and tasteless as it would be to a man of spirit, it give old jaundice-chops strength.

"Take my bloody word for it, mate," he said, putting the glass down, "I know my bloody business when it comes to cock linnets."

"Here, Tosher," the Old Cock shouted, "is there a big lady looking for me in the public?"

"No," shouted back the publican, his voice edged with the first whisky of the evening (the fourth of the day, Mrs. M. being in one of her niggling moods). "And don't shout," he shouted.

"I've spoken in public on singing birds," the yellow man complained, his brown eyes wide with indignation. "I'm on my jack jones when it comes to dickie-birds, and I don't care who knows it."

"You don't tell me?" the Old Cock asked, thinking poor dear Miss Weighty Waite, she didn't stand a dog's chance with that bird, but she kept on waiting. "Have a look at this." He pulled the gauntlet out of his pocket. "I'm the same way with armour. Spoken in public and private just like you, more than once. Have another."

"Lemon shandy," the man said. "Half. Rare old piece I would say." He held the glove in his hand like a bird, eighteen inches from his face.

"It's all coming back, you know," the Old Cock whispered in the bird-fancier's ear. "They never found nothing to beat it. I got a breastplate goes with this, must be half an inch thick. No stray sniper's gobs can pierce such a thing. Follow me?"

"Oh, yes?" the man replied, reaching down to the floor for his other cage. "You watch when I put the two of 'em together. The Dagenham Girl Pipers — nothing less." He brought the cage up onto the bar. The other little bird opened its eyes and looked straight up at the Old Cock. Then it twitched its head away as if any pupil of Miss Waite's just wasn't worth singing at.

Mrs. M. served them both, looking down her nose at the cages and the Old Cock, but that was nothing to go by because she had one of them

[191]

noses which you just couldn't help looking down, it being long and thin coming right up into the forehead with the eyes hung close to it.

Now the bird-man could see the Old Cock was genuinely interested, he relaxed a bit. "Confidentially," he said, "they do sing a bit on their own. Just as you might yourself, if you didn't have someone to talk to, talk to yourself like."

"I do all the time," the Old Cock said. "I think we all do, don't you? Specially on night-guard, about three in the morning when that bite is coming into the air and it's all quiet, so you know someone somewhere is up to something. You sort of mumble to yourself all kinds of stuff like bits of song and cursing the various officers, saying prayers for 'em we always called it. I wonder if the old armour has any warmth in it?"

"Exactly," the cock-linnet man said. "Same thing with the linnet. He'll mumble a bit from time to time on his own, same as you might yourself. But it don't compare with the full glory of his tiny treble when he takes all the stops out. Watch this." He pulled the cage over so that the one bird would be looking straight at the other bird as soon as he took his hand away. "Now," he said, and pulled it away.

The little birds twitched for a while, trying not to see each other. Then one gave out with a small warning peep. The other cock pretended he couldn't hear, his head jerking this way and that. "Chichichichit," sounded off the challenging linnet. "Tsooeet," replied the other, a bit doubtful-like.

"The anxiety note that is," the cock-linnet man explained. "He knows he's in for a bit of a battle and he don't like it."

"Tsooeet," shrilled the anxious bird. "Tsooo-eeet."

"Metallic," observed the linnet-master, "but less so than the twite and much less than the red-poll."

"Much less," agreed the Old Cock. "What's he then? Got the wind up? Got trousers full, old chap?" he asked the bird.

"Tsooeet-ooeett," the bird answered miserably.

"He don't want to fight it out," the man said. "He always was windy."

"And why not?" asked the Old Cock. "He's showing good sense. Why should he kill hisself? For what?"

"Makes a glorious show when they sing against each other, mate. Just listen to it," answered the man dreamily. The other bird, the brave one, was now going at it hammer and tongs, blowing itself up like a warbling pig trying to put the cowardly fellow out for the count.

The Old Cock called for a large whisky and downed it in one. Then another. He picked up an evening newspaper, drank the second whisky, stared at the linnet-master and deliberately placed the paper over the frightened linnet's cage.

"Tsooeet," called the bird, even more frightened.

"Don't worry, old fellow," the Old Cock said, "it's the Armistice. Cease fire! " he shouted at the other screaming monster. "Down arms, you murderous kite!"

The cock-linnet man tried to get the paper off the cage. "Turn it in," he kept saying as the Old Cock held him at arm's length.

"Never you mind about turn it in," the Old Cock said. "Give us another whisky, Tosh. This is the end of the contest, mate. Take off."

"Who are you then?" the bird-man demanded. "Who do you think you are? Who are you giving your orders to then?"

"To a dirty bird-hating tyke, that's who," the Old Cock answered, fiddling with the cage-door.

"To a louse who locks up free-living air-borne tiddlers for his sport. I been a member of Our Dumb Friend's League all me life and we are sworn to put down such evils as and when."

"They like to sing, you soppy old bastard," the linnet-man squeaked, struggling to get at the cage.

"Tsooeet-tsooeett," piped the loser bird.

"Chichichichichit," shouted the winner one.

"They don't know any different. It's their life," insisted the linnet-man. "That metal glove of yours is biting into my arm. Give over, do."

The knight-errant Old Cock pushed the little cage-door in, and groped inside for the captive bird. His hand found it, a fluffy shuddering heart, lifted it through and held it above his head.

"For Saint George and Merry England," he shouted, running up and down the bar, whipping up other people's drinks and downing them, the linnet-man jumping about trying to reach the hand that held the bird.

"Turn it in," shouted some.

"Leave my beer alone," cried others.

"A bar-thief," spat one fellow, "the lowest kind of scum."

"Give him back his bird," they all shouted.

"Chichichichit," sang the still caged linnet.

"Tsooeet," answered the muffled anxious bird in hand.

"He'll have to leave," Mrs. Metcalfe kept saying.

"You'll have to go," Tosher Metcalfe kept shouting.

"Stop him. He's barmy," they all hued and cried, several of them coming at the defiant Old Cock.

"Victory or death," he shouted. "They shall not pass." Unclasping his hand he threw the linnet up into the air above them all where it fluttered tsooeetting like mad. Then as they looked up he dodged through the swing-door under the bar.

"Out of here!" shouted Tosher, bundling the Old Cock through the bar door of the Public on the other side.

"Hands off!" shouted the Old Cock, then looking ahead saw suddenly the truth of all and fell silent. For there drinking milk-stout to his manly pint was La Goffin. And *He* was none other than that thief-in-the-night, that robber-baron of ill-repute, wooing her as hard as his

woos could go, fornicating Bates, the demon
adulterer of the sanitary department.

"Hands off," the Old Cock said again, quietly
now, his eyes grimly passing from her to him.

"I thought you was never coming," La Goffin
said uneasily. "Mr. Bates kindly asked me to join
him in one."

The Old Cock pushed Tosher's hand away and
walked forward.

"Your breath!" La Goffin said as he passed her.

"Get out, you drunken old out-of-work,"
Bates snarled.

"Out you go," Tosher said, coming up behind
him. "From now on you're banned. Understand?"

"Ruins the tone of the place," Bates said shift-
ily. "Shall we leave, my dear?" He fidgeted, looking away from the Old Cock.

Slowly, the Old Cock lifted his gloved hand
like a war-axe, then brought it down catching
Bates a straight left to the jaw. La Goffin
screamed. Several regulars seized him by the coat.
Tosher's hands were on his shoulders. Bates slid
heavily to the floor. "Knuckle-dustered!" someone shouted. The Old Cock give Bates' doxy one
killing look, then broke away.

He strode fast up the street, the fresh air entering his head at all points, till the cross-currents forced him to lean against a lamp-post for a second. Then he heard shouting behind him and started to run. It seemed he could get along faster if he flapped his arms and breathed out loud. "Tsooeet tsooeet," came his breath. "Tsooeet tsooeet." As he ran, the iron-bound gauntlet slipped off his hand and clanked on to the gutter-stone.

"Tssooeet," whistled the Old Cock. "Sod it. Tssooeet."

15

THE NEXT MORNING it was so quiet Arp thought everybody had been killed by bombs (a new silent kind) except him as usual. In the night these specials cut down through the black air not screaming nor conspicuous like those common types the last time, but (except for the rush of wind through their tails) silent. And silent as they hit the earth. And silently explode. And silently send the creeping bugs into all sleeping noses. And silently paralyse various parties young and elderly, all except immune Arp, who, as he dressed, thought it has all happened before, it will all happen again unless a better job of clearing up is made. Here we go again. And silently Arp went out to clear up the silent place.

But what a pleasant surprise, there were no corpses, which was hats off to the cleaning-up services and the speed with which modern science gets rid of the offending sights it makes. The building stood unshattered, the canteen was locked, the kitchens cleared of all except one pair of mouldering kippers which he washed off under the warm water tap now giving out ice-cold. At least if they was the only ones left he and the Old Cock will have a nice kipper break-fast. The Old Cock was expert with a kipper, not a fragment remaining on the hairy bones, a joy to watch him work.

But in the Old Cock's hut there was nothing disturbed, simply no sign of the old gentleman, which was funny because you would have thought nothing could have finished off that horny old toad. Doubtless the new specials was the finest job ever turned out by man. Arp stood for two minutes' silence in memory, but no smallest tear came because it was one of the things he always expected to happen, and often listened for, hence his occasional lack of atten-tion to the Old Cock's endless carry-on. Old Cock, Old Cock, they might have give you the last word, not knocked you off like any grey old porker while you snored.

As Arp turned away from the Old Cock's

empty shack, a lorry stacked high with office furniture came to a screaming stop, and Walt the property man looked out of the seat next to the driver's (so he must be on the debris team).

"Tara, Arpie," he said, "where's the Old Cock? Oh well, it was always too good to last. We left you a load of junk down by the big studio doors. Help yourself and good luck." He leaned back to the driver, "We don't want to get ourself a bad name being seen with the well-known bankrupt, Claygate Corst. Ta-ra, Arp." And they drove off.

So there were still a few left alive, including (by the grace of God) Mr. Corst himself, for here he came, dawdling between the sheds talking to himself and watching his long boat-shaped shoes.

"I done it before, I'll do it again," Corst was saying. "I ain't down yet by a long shot, not me, not Corst, you guys make a big mistake, I seen you in, I'll see you out, I was stabbed in the back on all sides, that bastard stole my little Roda from me, he stole my little girl, the dirty heel, that stinking lush Heinie ruined me, that lousy distributor betrayed me, betrayed is all you can call it, he and that wife, could I tell him about her, make his last few hairs drop out, let the whole

god-damn lot drop dead, they ain't seen the end
of it yet, no, not by a long shot, they ain't seen
the end of me, I been down before, plenty times,
but I always make out." And so on and so forth
in a shambling endless mumble, gone slightly
mad, Arp reckoned, with the great burdens of
his high office and the heavy mantle of leadership,
poor gentleman and war-lord, the last raid was
too much for him as indeed it would be for all
except the most experienced such as Arp, for
whom nothing could be so bad as it had already
been.

Ickabod, Ickabod (as the Old Cock were he
yet with us might say), so passeth the glory of
great Corst and his merry notions for getting rich
quick by the wholesale purveying of pictorial
lechery. For as the most boulder-headed among
you will have realised by now (being so far ahead
of Arp in quickness of understanding) Hundred
Per Cent American Films is a complete wash-out
due to under-capitalisation, labour problems, and
of course unbridled randiness and immoderate
boozing, not counting the fact Corst and his gen-
erals do not know their business from a hole in
the road. And indeed all but the most brainless
morons (Corst's fashionable word) will have

comprehended all this right from the outset. Indeed when that certain far-sighted Councillor said (right when the whole business was first mooted) give him a free month's trial and if worst comes to worst at least we get the place cleaned up for nowt, believe me he wasn't far wrong, for nothing much is changed by all our shouting. The glory that is Ancient Rome, tiddled up a bit, will resist the weather a little while longer than otherwise. The grandeur that is Westminster Abbey is a little restored with fresh plaster. The disrespectful hands have had their last knockings and all, all is passed except Corst the old show-man, no whip to crack and no one to crack it at, going through a temporary phase of barminess before he digests his disappointment preparatory to making his next assault upon that (for the time being) unfriendly whore, Fortune.

Watching Corst drifting about like an empty bottle in a sewer, Arp (without intending any disrespect) was forced to ask himself why should Corst be spared and the Old Cock carried off to a community grave, ditched in with a mob to whom he wouldn't normally pass the time of day unless they was relations. And furthermore, if Corst and Walt and the driver and himself had got away with it, why not others, or at least the Old Cock? Maybe there was some others about even now, at this moment looking around like him for their own particular mates and wondering why they should be spared and not them. If it was always going to end up like this, no one left in the world except a few strangers among the rubbish-dumps, why go on with the job? Why struggle to polish up rusty nails, why sift the clinker, why keep the pressed cardboard boxes dry, why wash the sack, why sort the ewes from the lambs on the hills of junk?

Arp sat upon the deep lowest step which led up to the great front doors (repainted dark blue for some reason) of Westminster Abbey and pondered, that's all you could call it, he definitely pondered. From where he sat he could see the nice Leaning Tower of Pisa job they was knocking up just before the plague carried them off. Ah, Ickabod, for the time being the pickings had been extremely good (it would be curmudgeonly not to admit that). Nevertheless, was it for this, to come down to this had it all occurred?

Forgetful as I am, Arp thought, if I forget you, Old Cock, may my right hand forget to know my left. If I do not hold you my best friend ever,

[204]

for all I know, my father, my mother, my wife, my nipper, may I never speak again. For still, after all this time, Arp still thought of himself as a speaking man, normal but with a poorish memory for certain things, a funny quirk which made you forget how to actually get the sounds out. If not, thought Arp, wouldn't I half shout from the rooftops the name of the Old Cock so they would hear of him, and (who knows?) if he still possesses the power to hear, maybe he himself will crawl back out of a trench somewhere, crawl again through no-man's-land, crawl back here to tell me once again a thing or two. I would climb the Leaning Tower of Pisa and call to him, thought Arp. In fact, he thought, I will actually, making no more bones about it, climb that very Tower so if the enemy is actually marching on us I will at least be warned and to a certain extent forearmed, and if not, let it be some small contribution to his dear memory.

Now the smiling Arp hauled himself up by his stubby fingers, pushed up with the toes of his knobbly boots, pulled at the uneven stucco with his fingernails (breaking two, the middle left hand and the tidgy right). The old lathes creaked and snapped. Old plaster broke away under the new and he dropped handfuls behind him and once looked down to watch it shower like hailstones. The Leaning Tower leaned as Arp, short order of springy muscle that he was, crawled up its rickety front, drawing the length of his body up, higher and higher. If he had dripped with water you might have thought him some kind of ratty animal living in the clay bank of a river and knowing its way around better than if it had brains to think and tongue to tell its thoughts.

So everyone in the world gets on with their private business. Here Corst bumbles to himself, plotting in his daft way to buy the Empire State Building and not enough do-re-mi in his pocket to acquire a second-hand mouse-trap. Here Arp doing the best he can climbing the Leaning Tower of Pisa by way of lament for the Old Cock. Here, half a mile up the road, Walt stopping the lorry to tell that very same Old Cock (bendy but jolly again after his ripe old night's sleep in a cat-alley) the die is cast, the party is over. He could have fallen over when the Old Cock tells him in broad terms how he has come unexpected into money of which remains some twelve pound cash even after the excesses of the night. Good luck, Old Cock, says Walt, though you don't seem to need it and Christ knows there ain't enough to go round. Good luck, Old Cock, all the same, says Walt, and departs into a different story.

Full of himself and his secret plan the Old Cock encounters by the gates of the once-again derelict studio the forlorn figure of Corst, picking his nose for inspiration and dying for a drink.

"A good coincidence, Mr. Corsir," says the Old Cock, putting out his hand to be shook, for a little money bringeth a great deal of pride and the Old Cock, his pocket full, is now a fair equal to his former masters.

Similarly Mr. Corst, brought a little low in spirits by his latest epic catastrophe and as short of friends as he is of lolley, thinks no more than twice before recollecting the democratic balderdashery of his background, and, lonely as a puffy cloud, grasps the outstretched grimy paw as if it was verbena-scented and emerged out of a fifty guinea suit.

"It's tough on all of us, old fellow," says Corst, a Southern-style colonel defeated by impossible odds. "But I want to thank you for your faithful service."

"No, thanks," replies the Old Cock. "Let's

leave the loyal service mulligatawny to the Pick-
lewaters of this world. I have simply done me
duty in all fairness to one who, if I may make so
bold, I look up to as one of nature's gentlemen."

"I thank you," grunts Corst, genuinely
touched. "If others had served me so loyally the
enterprise had come to a better port." He chokes
back a sob.

"How much," asked the Old Cock, squinting
calculatingly, seeing that this is the perfect moment. "How much will you take for the Nissen
hut? Cash. No nonsense."

Robber baron to the last as he was Corst knew
that there is a time to toughen up and a time to
be easy. In these circumstances he took a tenner
from the flush but business-like Old Cock who
at once made out a receipt on the back of the
very envelope the fateful redundancy notice had
arrived in, both businessmen forgetting (as is not
unusual among their ilk) that the Nissen hut in
question was not Mr. Corst's to sell with or without a receipt. But why be petty?

Now as Corst phones from a public call box
for a taxi to Town, planning as he does so his next
raid upon Fate and Destiny Incorporated, a new
burlesque production upon the very next con-

venient rubbish heap, so the Old Cock returns with swelling heart to Arp, finding him neither in shack, nor Nissen, nor sorting bottles, nor upon the dump.

"Arp," shouted the Old Cock as he trotted round and about. "Arp."

But Arp was off in one of his day-dreams and didn't hear.

When the Old Cock found him at last, stuck up on top of the Leaning Tower of Pisa, for gord's sake, he called up to him, "Arp, you silly old bugger, come down, you soppy old sod. Arp," he bellowed, "Arp."

Arp suddenly came round thinking, no that's wrong, no one's calling me. I'm calling him. When he looked down and saw it was the same bleary, beery, alive Old Cock it give him such a shock he fell over backwards, into the hollow centre of the Tower.

All the way down Arp fell, way down the Leaning Tower's long dark creaking throat, the weight of his body breaking the dry joists as he hit them, the rotten plaster sections dragged inward by the broken down-falling timbers, bumping Arp bit by bit backward (it seemed) down a tunnel. His hands grazed against the rough-cast walls and, he thought, we just have to wait to hit ground that's all, different again from a tunnel where you walk upright leaving a clatter behind you and still further back crumbled plaster, cracked spars, loose bricks, broken mortar, making the grey coat felting, the three-piece suite torn to pieces, the kapok stuffing all over, everything all over, and over all the dust settling. Where was it gone, the few yards of life? Dust on the rubble, rubble over the rubbish, and under the rubbish *nothing* sprinkled with blood from his torn and shaking fingers.

When the Old Cock got the plaster and lathes out of the way, Arp was on his knees scraping at the rubble with bleeding fingers. He was whispering over and over again, "Where are they, Mary, Micky, where are they, Mary, Micky, where, are, where, where, Mary, Mary, Mary."

But once the Old Cock lifted him out of the rubble he never said any more, just lay there in their very own receipted Nissen, his eyes turned to glass and his face white as broken plaster.

"Cheer up, Arp," the Old Cock said, as he tucked him round with a blanket. "We're rich, Arp," he said. But Arp, slow on the up-take as usual, just didn't want to know.

[210]

"You don't want to know, do you, Arpie?" the Old Cock said gently running his hands over Arp's ribs to see if anything was broke. "You just don't want to bloody-well know," he said, doing up Arp's shirt.

16

Even into late spring on the allotments the thick dirty brussel sprout stalks wait rotting to be chopped up and dug in to feed future lettuces whose last yellow leaves (mixed with old dried blood) bring on the new green autumn tomatoes which, though they never ripen in the quickly fading summer, at least make chutney to mature through the winter. The small stakes of earth wait to be dug over to sweeten in the sun, each guarded by a shack of clapboard or tin, cracked glazed salvaged window-frames thrown together in midget conservatory or summer-house style a bit fancy and painted a bottle-green. Held together with iron bed-heads (their brass knobs long lost) and bound by chicken wire, the allotments drag shaggily down to a tired meadow, and at their lower end the grass is already overrun, grown high as your knee.

Lying down here you smell the rank weeds and watch the ants scamper out of the bombardment of your breath. Between the roots they hide and hatch their tiny plots for survival, and as history goes to show, they survive. The small flies and the narrow creamy moths dart into their bushy pleasure-houses, do their business and drop dead unconcerned. You could be miles away from the rubbish-tip now officially full and closed down by the all-powerful council. You are far away (although not in an altogether different world) from the ramshackle studios once again empty, the recent whitewash already grubby in the bright spring-light, the temporarily made-good ruins back in their natural ruined splendour, flaking gently to dust in the sun. No estate agent (no matter how high-class) could argue that the lower end of the allotments was anything but desirable building land. To the lower end in the suddenly warm weather Arp and the Old Cock shifted their Nissen.

Back of the Nissen birds lived, linnets maybe, choral-singing enough to make the allotments into a meadow. They sang now as Arp, his back still a bit stiff (the old Cock said babies and barmies are made of rubber but it was still stiff), bent down to dip a salvaged brush into a biscuit tin of salvaged primrose oil-bound distemper.

"I reckon you'll just have enough there for the one coat, Arpie," said the Old Cock as he polished the breastplate of his armour with a knob of steel-wool. "What's your feelings on the matter, Arpie?" he went on, trying once again in his cunning way to get Arp to again talk. Arp turned and nodded because what need to talk even if you could, what need to try in case you can't, and if you tried and did, what find to say?

The Old Cock tied the breastplate to a coat-hanger and hung it on the door. Then he pulled at a stalk of grass so hard it came up in a clump. He nipped the stalk off, put it carefully between two teeth which happened to adjoin and sucked on it slowly.

"You know what we're going to have, Arpie, me old cock-sparrow," he hissed through the stalk. "When I collect the rest of me fortune from the thieving council, Arp, first thing we do is to cop ourselves two nice sets of false teeth. Lovely shining white teeth, Arp, so we can masticate our good grub and live like a couple of kings on our estate here. It's a good feeling to have a place of your own, Arp, ain't it, with a lovely

[214]

view and the smell of the veg growing away like mad, and a nice few bob in the Post Office to fall back on in case of need. We come out alright, Arp, though sometimes it looked like the dark clouds was here to stay, yet in the end they come through with silver linings for all, our own nice little detached residence in a rural setting, and snubs to Mr. Bloody Bates esquire. Soon as me claim comes through, Arp, remember, a couple of nice white solid ivory sets, none of your cheap plastic or bone, but only the best for yours truly and his handsome sparring partner. I won't be sorry to get rid of these flaming black bastards sticking up like five half-demolished chimney stacks in a gaping crater. Get a good set of teeth in your gob, Arp, and you look straightaway twenty year younger, specially in armour. Clickety click, clickety click, who's this coming along? Looks like John Boles the White Knight or rub in a spot of walnut juice and could be Valumtino the Black Knight hisself. Clickety click, clickety click, I loff you, Emily, cheese, cheese. Look at that flashing smile. More hygienic too, just stick 'em in a glass of water at night and start the day with a fresh clean feeling in your jaw. Crunch, crunch. Look, Arp, I'm gnawing a bone. Look here, Arpie, I'm chewing up the marrow from a lovely old marrow bone. Grr, grrr. Crunch, crunch. Here Fido, here Fido, good doggie."

On his hands and knees the Old Cock skylarked around snuffling at Arp's legs, sniffing the fresh paint drips on the ground, hoiking his back leg, finishing up by rolling in the grass, a puffing old tripe-hound.

"I should not have judged her too harshly, Arp. I reckon we might have made a go of it, Arp, you know, me and her," his voice wheezed from the grass patch. "Specially now I am coming into me just deserts. She got her own little house down Bermondsey way, you know. She's what they call a merry widow alright, I never saw such a behind on anything less than a horse in my life, as well as other good points. I'll give you a for-example. Nothing against a bloke taking a drink from time to time, which is essential in a spouse. Good sense of fun and game for it, without which you can shut up shop and go home. And cook, well I don't have to say nothing on that subject, you know yourself, Arpie, she is one of the all-time cooks of all time. What wouldn't I give for one of her specials tonight, all steaming on the table over a nice table-cloth, Arpie, with matching knives and forks. I definitely decided, Arp, we're going to buy ourself a table-cloth. Soon as I get me sponduliks we're going to buy a table-cloth and some flashy cutlery. If only women had a faithful heart."

He sat up in the grass, fished out of his pocket a split cigarette packet shopping list, dipped out a stub of pencil and licked the point.

"O-n-e t-a-b-l- c-l- that'll do to jog me memory. Yes, Arp, I reckon we might have made a go of it. Little house of her own in Bermondsey she's got. Formerly Goffin, I don't know what she was before. I didn't half cop that Bates a wallop, I can tell you."

The Old Cock pulled himself up from the ground. "It's no good, Arpie," he grunted. "It's no good at all. Look at it which way you like, she was the dearest lady I ever have the privilege and good fortune to meet. I should go up to her, all cock-a-doodle with confident proudness, not-withstanding I am just in receipt of a small matter of a redundancy notice, forget all that, forget all that, Emily, I tell her, this is no ordinary case of down on your uppers, this is me, bloody perhaps, Emily, but definitely unbowed and owed money. I forgive you, Emily. Let's have a go at the registry office caper. I'll get dressed."

He skilfully put the armour on, Arp assisting him. "Pity I lost the other gauntlet somewhere," he said, "but it's not my fault. That black swine Bates slandered her. She is no flighty old bag, but a real lady. I shall seek her by the tram to the far south of the river, through all of Bermondsey I shall seek, Arp, to tell her, Emily, do not look at the dirty shell of this old crab-louse before you. Do not be put off by vain thoughts of why don't he wash his neck and all that fancy pouffery. Have no fear for the future but give me your little hand in mine and we will fare forward together, looking not to left nor right, but straight ahead, your bits and pieces safe in the grip of one who, sometime a bit of a thief, sometime a bit of a liar, even once or twice a weeny touch of a coward (but everybody is no matter what horse-shit they drop you) but one (and I mean meself, Emily) who never has in all his years (no, better not refer to age and that), one who has never been known to have ponced on anybody his whole entire life, but has lived as he will die a true-blue soldier and gentleman of the other ranks and, dear lady, your personal knight of the — flaming piss-holes," he whispered suddenly looking up and ahead. "Suffering dogs and cats, Arp, look over there and say do me eyes deceive or is that the hated serge-draped carcase of that turd in pig's clothing, Bates. Pull out the barricades."

In double-quick time they had their barricade of requisitioned barbed wire and bed-heads pulled out. Peering through they saw it was indeed the loathed villain himself, his face blissfully black and blue with bruises, approaching their very territory. With Bates was a couple of dogs in police uniforms plus another filth-pot of the same ilk, a short bowler-hatted merchant he was, with mean ferret eyes and a curly pipe stuck in his cracked clock like a factory chimney gone cock-eyed. As the disgusting official crew (for you could smell the council on them a mile off) approached, the bowler-hatted beast could be heard belching complaints. Bringing up the rear a silent cloth-capped union official kept hisself to hisself.

"Definite offence," the bowler-hat was saying, "no two ways about it, definite breach of, definite case, definite example of breach of Town and Country Planning Act, no licence applied for, public land, placing building of temporary nature thereon, none forthcoming either, in such case, definite breach no two ways about it."

As he give his considered expert opinion it would have made you puke to see Bates' battered face grow oily with a look of goodie-goodie, got him by the shorts again.

"Quite so," replied Bates, the waxy magistrate's nark. "Quite so, oh dear me, yes, quite so," he drooled, the stool-pigeon's stool. "Additional to assault and battery officers," he squeaked, "additional charges officers. Including the assault and battery, seventeen charges."

The party of insurgent pan-handlers crept closer and stood silently watching. Then suddenly the cloth-capped one snapped, "What I think is unforgivable is not paying his Union dues for twenty-two years. Just forging the card. That's what I think is unforgivable. Taking twenty-five pounds of fellow-workers' money from the Union under false pretences. That's the unforgivable thing."

"Ay, ay," whispered the Old Cock, "the entire bloody bunch of balloons is up. Prepare for action." He pulled the vizor of his helmet down, then scuttled into the ditch and began to panther crawl forwards.

"I'll take the rekky," he whispered. "Pop down the field and borrow a horse. If I do not return in two hours, release the horse and evacuate the position." He reached up and gripped Arp's hand in his ungloved one for a moment, then moved off clanking faintly on his belly.

Arp watched the enemy forces gathering and whenever an enemy looked directly at him he stared straight back at that enemy. "Don't give any trouble," one of the rozzers shouted. "You're only making things worse." So that Arp started to collect what suitable bricks and other projectiles lying handy into a pile. He was arranging them neatly into a sort of pyramid, big ones as a base going up to smaller with the smallest on top when he heard the Old Cock hoarsely whispering from the ditch:

> "*John Wesley had a little dog*
> *He was so very thin*
> *He took him to the Gates of Hell*
> *And threw the bastard in.*

That's our pass-word. Where's the horse?"

The Old Cock pulled himself up over the ditch-side. "Where's the bleeding horse?" he asked again. "Can't I leave anything to you?" He fiddled with one of the bits and pieces of his armour which had broken loose. "And give us a lump of string to tie this bastard with," he said. "We'll have to have a change of plan. Where are they dug-in?" He squinted through the barricade. "Keep guard, corporal. If they make any movement, hold your fire. Got yourself proper fixed up there, Arpie?" he added, admiring the nicely arranged ammo. He gripped Arp's hand again and slunk off round the back of the Nissen.

"Let 'em come," Arp said in his head as he weighed a brick in his hand, a sneer of pride wrinkling his upper lip, over which he wished he had a moustache like the Old Cock to make a more military appearance. He chewed at his iron rations of bread and onion (the basic needs of a fighting man in the field, said the Old Cock).

On the other side of the barricade, the enemy was knotted together talking softly. Arp weighed the brick again and changed it for a heavier one. It was all he could do not to chuck it, specially when the bowler-hatted merchant looked at him.

"Fire! Fire, Arp! Keep lobbing them pineapples over!" the Old Cock's shout suddenly came from a little distance away.

As Arp lobbed the bricks over and the enemy retired to a safe distance shouting and holding up its fists, the Old Cock galloped into the encampment mounted on a pensioned-off white cart-horse. "Put me straight, matey," he puffed to Arp, his armour having slipped a bit and the weight tending to pull him sideways. In his right hand he held tight to a wooden paling pulled from the meadow fence.

"Up with the drawbridge," he shouted. "Pull the bloody bed-irons away, Arp, you daft-haporth. Heave away."

Arp heaved at the barricade but the old horse, over-excited by all the coming and going and feeling frisky for the first time since the brewery made him redundant, started to lurch forward.

"Here we go!" shouted the Old Cock levelling his wooden paling. "Up Fred Karno! Come and get it, you poxy dirty huns. No more trench war! Stop me and buy one! Here I come, you lousy whoresons!" He pressed his boots to the flanks of his mount and jangled down upon them.

"You'll pay for it!" shouted the cheated union cheat just before the Old Cock caught him a fourpenny one right up the backside.

"I always have," the Old Cock shouted back. "I always have paid for me pleasure and I always bloody well will," he yelled as he knocked the helmet off one purple bobby. "So long as he's got a hole in his backside the working man always pays," he shouted, pushing the other dog in uniform into the ditch before galloping off across the allotments after the receding figure of yellow-livered Bates, on whose body every hair was on end, soaked with cowardly sweat and lit up like candles to show him and all such pea-hearted officials the road to buggery, the lousy rotten man-eating bowler-hatted tiger-mice.

After making sure the enemy was routed Arp got a pail of water and washed out his smalls. As he spread them on the barbed wire to dry in the sun he watched the Old Cock totter back on his puffed and spavined mount. He was singing hoarsely, "My old man's a dustman." In his head Arp sang proudly back, "He fought in the battle of Mons."

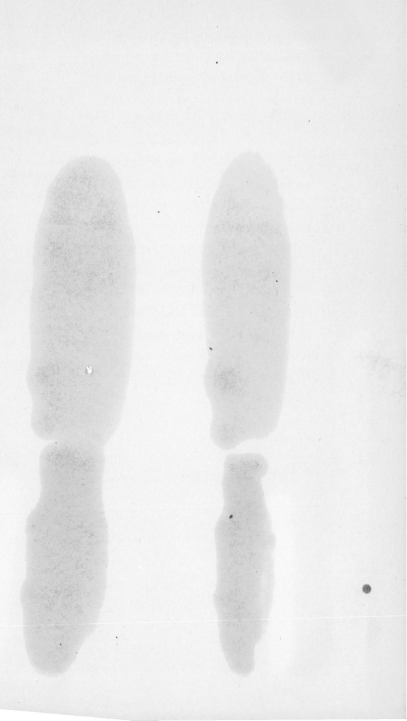

DATE DUE	

GAYLORD   PRINTED IN U.S.A.